The Darkness of the Sun

Cover design by Kent Grey-Hesselbein,

KGB Design Studio

Manchester, TN, USA

http://kghdesign.nvaazion.com/

The Darkness
of the Sun

by Rhonda St. Clair

with

Stan St. Clair

ISBN 978-1-935786-91-7

Printed in the United States of America by

St. Clair Publications

P. O. Box 726

Mc Minnville, TN 37111-0726, USA

http://stan.stclair.net

CONTENTS

The Darkness of the Sun

DEDICATION

It is my desire to dedicate this book to some special people in my life who have been great inspirations to me for many years.

First, my husband, Stan St. Clair, who inspired, encouraged and aided me in writing this book. His love and faith in me has been my hope and strength every day for almost 16 years.

Second, my mother, Doris (Peggy) June Jacobs, who gave me life and is one of the strongest women I have every known.

Thirdly, my daughter, Angela Dawn (Watson) Brown, who was my reason for living for many years who loved me no matter what I did; of whom I am very proud for the wonderful woman, wife and mother she has become.

Next, for my grandchildren, Louis Alexander (Alex) Brown and Abigail (Abby) Denyse Brown who have given me love and joy beyond belief.

These are very important people who I love very much and am thankful to God for their presence in my life.

CHAPTER ONE

Bella Fontaine stood immobilized, her hypnotic green eyes transfixed upon the gripping spectacle in the heavenly realm before her. The polarized Typhoon sunglasses sheltered her vision, blocking all but the most miniscule glare of the torrid rays caused by the sun's gradual entrapment beyond the brave parading moon.

A dedicated nurse in the field of Pediatric medicine, she had cautiously saved every available dollar from her part time job at the doctor's office in Maryville, Tennessee, where she relocated in 2006, to make this grand trip of her dreams.

It was July 11th, 2010, and Easter Island was everything that she had ever dared dream it might be. Known to the original natives as Rapa Nui, this small slice of heaven is extremely remote, located at the southeastern most point of the Polynesian triangle between Hawaii and South America. Widely famous for 887 extant monumental statues, called "moai," carved by the early inhabitants, Bella had read with rapture of their mysterious aura. The Rapa Nui National Park swallows up a large percentage of this virgin isle.

Now, as the tiny circle which remained of the sun's glory shouted out around the rape of the lunar body embracing it, chills permeated the length of Bella's slender spine.

My life, she thought, *has been like the darkness of the sun!*

"Bella Fontaine! You come here this instant and tell me where you've been!" her mother's earnest booming voice rang in her tender young ears as if she had used a bull horn. "I've been looking all over town for you!"

Bella's mom, Janine Fontaine, was a stunning, elegant lady, and very well-known in the small town of McMinnville, Tennessee. But part of her fame was her dominating personality and the fact that she was abusive to her daughter.

Bella dashed into the house, past her mother. Janine's arm plunged forward and grabbed

Bella's silky light auburn hair, pulling her roughly into her bosom.

"You answer me, young lady! Where have you been? And you better not lie. I'll know if you're lying!"

As the salty tears welled up in Bella's sensitive eyes from the intense pain of her hair being nearly jerked out by the roots, she managed to speak. "Mom, I've been over at Maggie's to tell her good-bye and give her our new address. She's been my best friend for the past two years, and I wanted her to know how much I'm going to miss her. We agreed to stay in touch."

It was a dark, gloomy rainy day and a horrible one for moving, but the sadness filled Bella's heart to know she was leaving her friends behind and the only town she had ever known.

Bella and her mom were moving to East Tennessee where Janine's mother was born—Maryville, south of Knoxville, at the base of the majestic Smoky Mountains.

Bella had known Maggie Denise Williams since they started the first grade at City

Grammar School. Both girls were small in stature, quiet and timid, and slow to join in play with the other children. They had met on the playground the first day of school, and hit it off right away. The girls actually had a *lot* in common. Red hair, freckles, green eyes and bony legs made them look more like sisters than merely friends. The two did everything together after that and now they were being separated. This tragic turn of events was almost unbearable for the inseparable girls. They had both been crying for days now.

"Will you get in here and help me pack? Your things are thrown all over the place and you're going to have to find them and do your own packing!" her mom screamed. "There's stuff all over the floor in your room! You're proving what an ungrateful little brat you are by treating your things so badly! You don't deserve nice things."

Bella did have some expensive toys, furniture and clothing that family members had given her through the years. *Was her mother right?* She looked down at the beautiful ornate porcelain doll with the blonde locks streaming down her back. She was outfitted in a red velvet Victorian dress with long black stockings and matching patent leather shoes. She stood approximately two feet tall, and Bella loved her so much. She had been a fifth birthday present from her Aunt Toni.

Also the huge, stately Victorian-style dollhouse filled with period furniture and tiny figurines of the house's inhabitants. It was a bright lemon yellow, and stood eighteen inches tall with a length of twenty-four inches. Actual plush yellow carpet served as floor covering, with tiny mosaic tiles in the bathroom and kitchen. It was so authentic that it seemed like the perfect home to Bella — one in which she had always imagined living. These two magnificent objects were her most prized possessions. The dollhouse was a gift from her dad before he had moved out when she was yet four.

As Bella stood gazing at the dollhouse, she could reminisce about the days when she and her father would pretend to be lavishly wealthy people living in that house, enjoying their fanaticized life together. She missed her dad so very much. Why had he left her and her mom? She had not heard one word from him since that ghastly day. People in town who knew him said he was working out on the outer banks of North Carolina. Joseph Fontaine had been a very prominent medical doctor in McMinnville, and Bella had been told that he had met a nurse at the hospital with whom he had fallen in love, and the two had left together.

Janine had made a tacit attempt to project the appearance that she had loved her husband, but Bella knew the truth—she didn't know how to show love to anyone, not even Bella. She never received encouragement and praise, only neglect and criticism.

As Bella began to pack her belongings, she felt the sadness build deep inside of her. She so wished that her father could be there to give her one of her favorite "Fontaine" hugs. He would hold her and tell her in no uncertain terms how much he loved her. *But why did he leave me?* The thought seemed rhetorical—it had no escape or answer which she felt acceptable. *Doesn't he love me anymore?*

She carefully gathered up all the small toys which she had accumulated over the years and placed them gingerly in the big box which the moving company had provided for them. Then she began placing the dollhouse paraphernalia into small boxes with tight-fitting lids and set them in the large box. The priceless porcelain doll was then wrapped in tissue paper and plastic and placed within a box that was padded with soft cushioning on the inside.

Mrs. Fontaine opened the door to Bella's room quickly and startled Bella so badly that she jumped from reflex.

"Aren't you finished yet? We don't have all day!" she snapped. "The moving van will be here in an hour. Now hop to it, young lady!"

"Yes, Mama." Bella felt terribly tense. Her heart was splintering into a thousand pieces.

But her mother had told her when she started crying, "Now straighten up. You're too old to act like that." She didn't seem to care how Bella felt, and how badly her heart and soul were torn apart. Bella tried to understand how her mother must have felt about loosing her dad. Bella silently cried from her inner core, *Daddy, please come back. I need you!*

Her mom had the timing down pat. In about an hour the moving van pulled up in front of the house. It looked like a gigantic monster coming to collect its prey. As far as Bella was concerned, everything she owned would be devoured by that monster in a short time and delivered to a place she really didn't want to go.

The only reason she found some small amount of respite in the situation was that they would be living with Grandma Bailey until Janine could ferret out a job. She loved Grandma very much and knew that Grandma had genuine care for her. She was a very kind, gentle, and loving person and everybody loved Grandma. Bella was confident that she could be happy there.

Four strong, muscular men jumped out and began lifting the furniture and setting it on the truck one piece at a time. She noticed that at least they were being careful in their arrangement of it in order not to scratch or dent anything. The containers holding fragile items were loaded last, with great caution.

The big monster truck's mouth shut and Bella felt the emotion of sadness rising from her inner being and tears begin to flow. This was the only house she had lived in; the neighborhood, though it was an aging one, was where her friends and the people she loved lived; the big brick church on the corner of Donnell and Spring Streets with the stately bell tower was the place she had learned about Jesus.

Janine noticed the tears streaming down Bella's face.

"Now there you go again! Quit your blubbering!" she said, a grimace paving the way for her tirade. "You're too old to act like that! Now dry your tears and I don't want to see this happen again!"

Bella laggardly stopped crying, but she could still feel her heart imploding.

As Janine pulled the car slowly out of the driveway, following the huge truck, Bella stared back to see the house disappearing in the distance. Inwardly the words rang forth, *Daddy, how will you know where to find me when you come back? Oh, how I miss you so!*

The trip to Maryville was only a couple of hours, but Bella was so emotionally exhausted, she slept the entire trip.

"Wake up, sleepyhead. You've slept away the whole trip. We have lots of work to do."

At that moment, the BIG monster truck along with the car carrying Janine and Bella, pulled up in front of Grandma's house. It was an old frame farmhouse, large enough to accommodate ten people, but Grandma had lived there by herself since Grandpa died seven years earlier. Bella didn't remember her Grandpa since she was only one year old when he passed, but she had spent pleasant times with her Grandma on several occasions.

The City of Maryville was a small town in Blount County, Tennessee, established in 1795 by the Act of the General Assembly of the Territory South of the Ohio River. Seven Commissioners were appointed to obtain fifty acres of land and therefore, divide it into lots and sell them with the proceeds to be used for construction of a courthouse and jail. The abundance of springs in the area for water supply was one reason for locating the town there. Maryville was named in honor of Mary Grainger Blount, wife of the Governor William Blount. The county was named in honor of the governor himself. Tennessee became the sixteenth state to join the union only a year later, on June 1, 1796.

Since 1919 it had been a twin town to Alcoa, home of the aluminum giant.

As Bella swung open the back door of the stunning two-tone black and silver 1958 Chevy, she was overly excited to see Grandma. At the same time, Grandma opened the huge screen door, and ran across the rickety porch into Bella's extended arms. Bella's heart burst with joy to see her again. Her hugs felt so warm and gentle, like those of an angel.

Grandma Bailey was a short, thin lady with very gray hair that she wore short at the nape of her neck. She had worked hard on the small farm which she and Grandpa Bailey had owned since they had married almost 30 years ago. Although small in stature, Grandma was plenty strong. Raising goats and pigs had been their livelihood, but now with Grandpa gone, she had found it very difficult to manage. Her finances were suffering so she found it necessary to sell the livestock. Bella was disappointed but she found out later that she had kept the Palomino, named Molly that Grandpa had cherished as a colt. Molly had been on the farm for many years and she was like part of Grandma's family. Because she was very gentle, many of the nearby children had ridden her numerous times. But Bella had always been too young and was forbidden to do so. Now she could hardly wait to ride Molly since Janine had said she was now old enough.

The hour was late when Bella and Janine arrived and not much was wasted on conversation before retiring for the night. The air outside was muggy with a soft, mellow breeze, but the atmosphere was very relaxed with the crickets cheerily chirping and the frogs monotonously croaking in the darkness. In a short time, the household was peaceful and filled with blissful sleep.

Morning seemed to come quickly, but Bella was awakened with the enticing aromas of coffee and bacon. She pulled herself up out of bed and pranced down the stairway which was coated by a sea of blue plush carpet. Janine and Grandma were in the kitchen having their a.m. cup of coffee. As Bella entered the massive, country kitchen, she couldn't help but notice the remarkably large cook stove, alive with a sparkling fire fueled by wood, kindled in the belly of that ornate range. It was superbly built, possibly in the 1930s, and the food cooked there was just as grand. From the oven, Grandma drew a long pan of homemade biscuits. "Cathead" biscuits, she called them. They were huge, flaky, and golden on the crest. As she opened them, the steam arose and the aroma permeated the room. Now this was what Bella had always imagined as "the warm feeling of home."

CHAPTER TWO

As the remainder of the summer flew quickly by, Bella knew that she would not forget that blissful time spent on the farm. Grandma Bailey grew a variety of vegetables in her garden and Bella enjoyed gathering them and helping her mother and grandmother prepare them for the fascinating canning process. They would gleefully toil in energetic synergy from dawn till dusk.

As the first day of school approached, Bella was full of anticipation. She questioned how many children would be in her class; the ratio of girls versus boys; how would they accept her being an outsider. This fear welled up inside her and she was overly anxious by the time school started.

It was a bright sunny morning the first day of class and Bella woke up full of enthusiasm. But not for long.

"Get yourself out of that bed, you lazy girl! You don't have much time before the school bus will be here. Snap to it!" Janine yelled as she darted into Bella's room that morning. "You have to go to school and I don't want to hear any of your nonsense."

Again, as usual, Janine was brashly harsh and didn't attempt to understand her fears. Bella climbed out of bed, hopped into her clothes quickly, and ambled downstairs.

"How is my darling little 'school' girl this morning? You look so pretty in your new dress," Grandma complimented.

Janine interrupted promptly with a snicker under her breath, "Oh, Mom, don't tell her that. It will go to her head. She's just a normal-looking eight-year-old girl. A bit on the ugly-side, if you ask me."

Grandma and Bella looked at each other with melancholy on their faces to the point of tears. Janine knew exactly how to stick a cold dagger through Bella's tender heart just when she was beginning to feel a wee bit better about herself.

Bella was a beautiful, green-eyed, red-haired, freckle-faced little girl, far from ugly. She had a very sweet personality and everybody loved her that truly knew her. Her mother was an only child with an alcoholic father and an overprotective mother. She was a spoiled brat that was not capable of loving her child, or even her husband. Bella knew that was why her father left her mother. He was a very loving man and had to have someone to love him, too.

"But I love you, Daddy, and I really need you to come back and love me. Please God, help him hear me, wherever he is," Bella prayed every night. She knew God would hear her and lead her father back home.

As the school bus approached the house, Bella reluctantly strolled down the long driveway to board it. Several children were already on the big yellow bus as the door swung outward and she ascended the two steps and eased down the aisle. She stopped and sat down behind a small, blonde-haired girl who appeared to be about her own age.

The young lass looked back and spoke to her softly. "You can come up here and sit with me if you want. We will be going to the same school so we'll see each other a lot. My name is Kathy McCormick. I live just down the road from your grandmother. My family has known her for a long time. Are you going to be staying in Maryville for a while?" Bella could tell that she and Kathy were going to be friends. She was a very delightful girl and had a beautiful smile.

Bella shrugged her shoulders. "I guess so. I really don't know," she said hesitantly.

The girls were silent the rest of the trip to school, but they did make it a point to sit close to each other in class and play together during recess. Kathy had several friends in school and she introduced Bella to them. Bella found them all very nice, but she liked Kathy the best.

Kathy had two brothers, Jake and Justin, but they were older. Jake was ten and Justin was twelve. They liked to bully the little kids on the bus to the point that the bus driver had to discipline them almost every day. Bella could see that she wasn't going to like them. They bullied Kathy all the time and Bella didn't like that. She could see how it disturbed Kathy.

Kathy's family was much approved by Grandma Bailey but Janine had negative things to say about them, of course. She knew Kathy's mom and said she was very "flirty" with the boys when they were in high school together. But she had changed and everybody in the neighborhood was aware of that. Mr. and Mrs. McCormick were very happy together and everyone could tell how deeply they loved each other. Janine had to find fault in everyone's happiness and Bella understood that.

Bella was right. She and Kathy became very close friends as the school year progressed. They told each other everything. Kathy, along with Jake and Justin, would come over to Grandma's and go horseback riding on Molly often. Bella loved sharing the graceful Palomino with her friends and she was such a gentle horse, all the children loved her. This began to alter the boys' actions toward Bella. She was beginning to love the farm and all her new friends. She even enjoyed her new school, Sam Houston Elementary.

Bella hadn't heard from Maggie in McMinnville for quite some time and decided to write another letter to her anyway. Grandma said she would help, so one night they did just that. She mailed the letter the next day. But in about a week it came back marked "Return to Sender." She didn't understand what that meant. Grandma explained to her that signified that the person receiving the letter didn't want it and sent it back or it could mean that Maggie no longer lived at that address. Bella's ninth birthday was coming up and she wanted to see if Maggie would come to her party. Now Bella was very hurt and disappointed and ran to her room in tears. Janine overheard the commotion and came to see what was happening. Grandma gently explained it to her, but Janine felt no pity. She pushed open the door to Bella's room and snapped at her, "Why do you want Maggie here anyway? You've made new friends now. Just forget about her!"

Bella was barely able to answer. "I know Maggie is angry at me because I left. I guess she's made new friends too and doesn't want me as her friend anymore!"

As time went by, Bella grew to accept the fact that Maggie no longer was her friend and she had lost touch with her. She never heard from Maggie again. But she remained in her prayers.

Oh, Lord, don't let Maggie be mad at me. I love her so."

CHAPTER THREE

Many years had flown by as a shooting star in the darkness of a country midnight. Bella had come to call Maryville and the farm "home". Janine had taken a good many types of employment since they had been there, but finally, she was offered substantial secure employment at Baptist Hospital in Knoxville. As Director of Nursing she would receive the best salary she had ever made. Although Bella and her mom could have moved into their own house, they chose to remain with Grandma Bailey. Janine thought it best since Grandma was getting older and needed someone to care for her. Being a nurse, and her daughter, Janine felt that she could do better than anyone else in that role.

Now Bella was sixteen and growing into a beautiful young lady. Some of her freckles had faded somewhat but her green eyes still sparkled like emeralds and her red locks hung in soft, bouncy curls down her back.

She was also becoming interested in dating and with her beauty the boys certainly were noticing her.

One night while she and Kathy were attending a basketball game at their school, they noticed an unusually handsome boy sitting all alone in the bleachers. As they approached him, they could see he was around seventeen years old. Dark hair, slender build, and deep brown eyes made him very attractive to Bella.

"Hi, my name is Bella Fontaine and this is my friend, Kathy McCormick. We attend school here." Bella had lost her childish shyness. "Do you mind if we sit with you?"

The boy smiled and motioned for them to sit by him. "Which team are you supporting, the Wildcats or Rebels?" Bella asked, hoping it was the Wildcats since that was her school team.

"By the way, my name is Thomas James. I'm supporting the Wildcats."

Bella grinned with excitement. She knew she was going to like this boy.

When the ballgame was over, with the Wildcats winning 85-60, Thomas asked for her phone number and permission to call her. Bella gave her number to him but said she would have to ask her mother's permission before he could call. He understood and said he would find a way to contact her later. Bella went home and told her mother about Thomas and the agreement they had made.

"What do you mean you gave your phone number to some strange boy? Are you crazy? Don't you know boys only want one thing? They'll make you fall for them and then hurt you. You're old enough to know better than that! Don't tell me I didn't warn you, and NO, he doesn't have my permission to call you!!"

Bella sighed. She didn't know how to reach Thomas to tell him he couldn't call her so she would just have to wait until she could see him again.

A few days passed and then while Bella was walking down the hallway at school one day, she glanced up and saw Thomas standing at his locker some distance away. Hurriedly, she made her way toward him.

"Thomas!" Her yell was bathed in excitement.

As he heard her voice, he turned and saw her comely form approaching. "Hi, Bella." His look was one of sudden surprise.

"I was afraid I wouldn't see you again," she said, "and I wanted to tell you what happened when I got home and asked my mom if you could call me. She said 'No', but now I know we can see each other at school."

Thomas said he understood. "We can sit together at lunch and maybe talk before and after school. Would that be okay with you?"

Bella smiled with approval as her heart was pounding. "That would be GREAT!!! We can also see each other at ballgames."

Bella was a very intelligent girl and was making excellent grades. Janine and Grandma were very proud of her, even though Janine couldn't express it. The principal told her that if she kept up the good work, she could graduate with a scholarship. She decided to work very hard and do exactly that.

CHAPTER FOUR

One Tuesday morning while Bella was in English class concentrating on what the teacher, Mrs. Davis, was presenting, she was called out by the school principal, Mr. Langley. He said it was an emergency and she was to call her grandmother immediately.

"Meet me in front of the school in fifteen minutes." Grandma's voice on the phone was tense. "You need to come home now. Your mother needs you."

"What is it, Grandma?" Bella's tone reflected her overt fear.

"I can't explain over the phone, Bella. You just need to meet me in fifteen minutes."

Bella hung up and did as she was told. She had to sign out in the office and then go outside to wait. Grandma was there on time and as Bella climbed into the car, she noticed that Grandma was in tears and in emotional upheaval.

"What's going on?"exclaimed Bella.

"Your mother has been in a bad car accident," Grandma said hesitantly. "The hospital called and told me she was hit by a drunk driver who ran a stop sign at the crossroads just five miles from the house. She was taken there and treated for head and chest injuries. She's in serious condition, Bella, and is in the emergency room. We're going there now."

Bella couldn't believe this. It was as if what she was hearing were in a tunnel. She was riddled with shock. She just couldn't lose her mother, and Grandma couldn't lose her daughter, either. She broke down in uncontrollable tears. *What would her mom look like?* she wondered. *Would she even be able to see her? Would her mom know she was there?*

As she and Grandma approached the ER, all the nurses were huddled in a group discussing Janine's condition. One of them opened the door to the ER and led them to her bedside. Bella's heart sank as she viewed her mom unconscious, attached to monitors and machines. Nurses were coming in and out taking her vital signs and attending to her. Her head was plastered with bloody bandages; her face with lacerations that had many stitches which would obviously leave indelible scars.

As Bella stood there watching her mother close to death, tears began to trail down her cheeks.

Grandma moved close and put her arms around her. "Speak to her, Bella," Grandma whispered. "She can hear you and know you are here."

So Bella edged closer, took her mother's hand, and whispered softly, "Mama, I'm here. It's Bella and I love you, Mama. Don't leave me, please!" She couldn't help but submit to the rush within, her sobs gushing vigorously forth. This time Janine could not answer harshly and say something negative, but Bella would rather have heard that than see her mother laying there near death.

The nurse walked into the room and told them they would have to leave. They were to go to the waiting room until the doctor could talk to them.

Bella and Grandma reposed in silence as they pondered on this situation and prayed together for God to help Janine have the strength to pull through this unbearable trauma. But they both knew that God's will was to be done in all matters.

Bella glanced around as she heard someone call her name.

"Bella, how is your mom?" There stood Thomas, holding flowers that he extended to her.

"She's in bad shape. Thanks for asking and thanks for coming."

"I heard about it at school and knew I had to come and see how you were doing." Thomas looked at Grandma, "Hi, Mrs. Bailey, how are you?" Then his gaze returned to Bella without waiting for a response. "This is such a horrific accident and I'm sorry your mother is going through this. They said the driver of the other car was drunk. They do have him in jail at this time because it is not his first offense. It was a stranger from Knoxville and not someone from here in Blount County. He'll have to live with this the rest of his life."

Bella hugged Thomas and began to sob again as he held her closely. "I'm so glad you're here," she said. "We don't know the prognosis yet. The doctor hasn't talked to us. We're waiting to hear from him. "

Just then Dr. Anderson walked into the waiting room. "Are you the Fontaine family?" he asked.

"Yes," Bella said as she stood up and approached the doctor.

Dr. Anderson spoke quickly, "I'm sorry but Janine is going to have to go to surgery. Her brain is swelling from the injuries and we have to relieve the pressure and see how much brain damage it has done. Do we have your permission to do surgery? We need you to sign a consent form. Mrs. Bailey, you will have to do this since Bella is underage."

Grandma signed the consent form. "Please do all you can for her." Her voice was quivering.

For what seemed like hours, Bella, Thomas, and Grandma decided to stay in the waiting area.

Finally, Dr. Anderson walked into the room with deep sadness in his eyes. "I'm so sorry but Janine didn't survive the surgery. There was just too much damage to the brain. Her lungs collapsed also and it was beyond our control to help her. I am terribly sorry."

After he said that, he turned and walked out leaving them to bask in utter shock. Grandma fainted and fell to the floor. Bella bent over her and put a cold cloth on her forehead. Within minutes, Grandma was waking up. Then she began to sob hysterically. Bella took her hand and tears began to stream down her face.

"Oh, Grandma, why did this have to happen? We've been praying for God to let her live. Why did He do this? How are we going to go on without her?" She paused, realizing that Grandma had lost her husband and now her daughter. How can she be strong enough to survive this? Bella's heart was really breaking for Grandma right now. She was suffering also by realizing she just lost her mother.

Oh, Dad, where are you and why can't you be here? I really need you now, Bella said to herself. She thought that losing her dad was the worst thing that could ever happen to her, but right now, the death of her mother had that topped. *This is unbearable!!*

Grandma regained control of her emotions, looked at Bella and took her hand.

"Bella, we don't know why God permits things to happen. He has a reason that we can't understand, but He will give us the strength to get through this. He always does."

Thomas reached out to Bella and Grandma and took them in his arms to comfort them. He was such a compassionate young man and Bella loved him for that.

"Anything I can do to help with the arrangements, please let me know," Thomas reassured her.

The next few days were unduly stressful and heartbreaking for the family. Thomas and Bella tried to relieve the burden from Grandma by making the funeral arrangements. Janine had acquired several friends in Maryville and co-workers at the Baptist Hospital in Knoxville where she was employed.

Bella also thought about friends of her mother's in McMinnville. She looked for the phone directory from that area and began to dial the phone. Although several of them had left McMinnville, she found some of her closest friends still there. Of course, they were all sorry to hear about the accident and told her that they would be at the funeral to say their goodbyes. All of a sudden, Bella remembered Maggie's mother, Mrs. Williams. She thumbed through the directory and found her number and began to dial.

"Hello," said the voice on the other end.

"Is this Mrs. Williams?" Bella was excited that she had reached her. "I don't know if you remember me, but this is Bella Fontaine. Maggie was a friend of mine when we were young. My mother and I moved to Maryville. I lost contact with Maggie after a short time. It occurred to me that she might have been angry with me for leaving. Do you remember me?"

"Yes, Bella, I do, but Maggie wasn't angry at you for leaving. She understood and was so happy every time she received a letter from you. But I have some bad news, Honey.

Maggie was hit by a car crossing the street in front of our house when she was nine years old. She died instantly. She missed you so much and was heartbroken when you left. She did make some new friends, but never forgot you. She hoped every day you would come back to McMinnville."

Bella again was stunned. Who else was she going to lose? "Oh, I am so sorry, Mrs. Williams. I would have wanted to say my goodbyes."

"I apologize for not getting in touch with you, but the grieving was unbearable for me for a long time," Mrs. Williams remarked regretfully. "My health is now suffering for it. Bella, I miss her so much. Her father and I divorced after that and I have been by myself just trying to make ends meet."

Bella suddenly realized why she called Mrs. Williams. "Oh, I almost forgot why I called. A few days ago my mother was in a car accident and died. I knew there were people she knew in McMinnville that would want to know and I thought of you."

"Oh, Bella, I am so sorry for you and your Grandma. Give her my sympathies. I know how hard it is to lose a child. But my health is so bad I don't think I could make the trip there. Remember my prayers and love are with you and your family. Again, know you have my sympathies from the bottom of my heart."

"It was so nice talking to you again, Mrs. Williams, although we only had bad news for each other. You take care of yourself and I'll keep in touch with you and see how you're doing," Bella said, regretting that she hadn't contacted her before now.

Bella finished the arrangements. Her heart was full of grief and would be for a long time, but she had to be there for Grandma.

Daddy, where are you and will you know about Mama and come to tell her goodbye? Bella whispered softly. She had never heard from her dad and even began to wonder if he was still alive. She heard through the hospital grapevine that he had moved around from town to town after getting a divorce from his second wife, the nurse he left her mother for, after only five years of marriage. Nobody seems to know where he is now. He went to Europe to work with a mission over there for a while.

"Lord," Bella prayed, *"please hear my prayer and bring my dad back to me someday."*

Bella and Grandma survived the funeral but the gnawing grieving didn't subside. They went home together after the service, held each other close and poured out the tears they had held in their hearts so long. Janine would be missed terribly by many friends and family. In spite of her faults, she was the strength that had held the family together since Bella's dad left. Even though her mother had spoken harshly to her, Bella loved her with all her heart and rued the fact that she did not get a chance to say goodbye.

The funeral was lovely with many beautiful flowers from friends and family all over Tennessee. It was a bright, sunny day in the spring of the year. Janine always loved the spring with the birds singing and all the plants coming alive after the winter's demise. She was buried beside Grandpa Bailey in the local town cemetery where numerous family members had been laid to rest.

CHAPTER FIVE

As the kingly sun crept out from behind the captor moon on Easter Island, tears flowed down Bella's smooth, rosy cheeks at the remembrance of her mother's untimely passing. Now she must get her mind on the next leg of her trip.

The lush rainforest of the tropical paradise around her seemed in stark contrast with the reality of her dark past.

But she could not escape the rush of memories which haunted her any more than she could elude the dream that drove her onward...the hope of finding her estranged father.

The next two years following the loss of her mother had passed quickly and it was time for Bella to graduate from high school. She and Kathy were so excited because they had both won scholarships. Kathy was going to attend Furman University in Greenville, South Carolina, but college seemed only a dream to

Bella. They hated the separation but knew it was for Kathy's future. Thomas was remaining in Maryville and had employment at the local post office. They all agreed to stay in touch through writing letters often.

"Bella," Grandma said to her one day, "I'm going to have to sell the farm and that means Molly will have to be sold also." Bella's heart sank. "Honey, we just can't make it on my small Social Security income and it's just getting to be too much for me to handle. I want you to go on to college as soon as you can and get your nursing degree, if that is still what you want to do. After giving it a lot of thought, I decided we might move back to McMinnville since the cost of living isn't as much there. What do you think?"

Bella was surprised but excited in the same moment. "Grandma, I'm sure you know what is best for you. That sounds like a good idea." She didn't want to leave her Grandma like this. After all, she had lost her only child and now she was losing the farm she had with Grandpa. Bella knew her Grandma was a strong lady but this had to hurt her immensely. Bella had never given up the thought that her dad may come back to McMinnville some day and her already being there would be great. So Bella and Grandma planned to move as soon as the farm was sold.

A local businessman heard about the farm being for sale and came by to speak with Grandma. He said he had been wanting to buy a farm to start a bed and breakfast inn around that area. After inspecting the premises, he was totally amazed at the asking price. He had also wanted to include horseback riding at the B & B and offered to buy Molly. Being that she was so gentle with children, he was eager to get her. Shockingly, the man offered her much more than what the property was appraised at and naturally she took it. But he had a bit of an ulterior motive. Since this was the spring season and he wanted to have the B & B ready to receive guests by midsummer, he asked if he could take possession the end of May. The agreement was made and Bella and Grandma started the preparations for moving.

Thomas found out about Bella's moving and made it a point to stop by one day and help with the packing. He was deeply disappointed to see her go, but knew they would keep in touch. They had grown very close, but only as friends.

The two weeks flew by and time was upon them for the move back to McMinnville. Mixed emotions filled Bella's heart and head. Grandma had done some searching in the local newspaper, the Southern Standard, and found a small house for them on Spring Street. It being less roomy, they had to store a lot of the furniture in a mini warehouse until they could decide what items they wanted to keep and what to sell. It was a huge adjustment for them. But they knew Grandma had made the proper decision for both of them.

After the unpacking was concluded and Bella felt comfortable leaving Grandma by herself, she went for a drive in the '58 Chevy Impala she had inherited from her mom. She found herself going back to the old community she had lived in before they moved to Maryville. After all, it wasn't that far from their new house. The area hadn't changed much but most of the people she knew had left because of the economy. They had to go up north to find jobs.

Without much delay, she went by the house where Maggie and her mom had resided. When she went to the door and knocked, a tall, well-built, sun-bleached blond young man, around twenty-one years old, answered the door. Immediately, Bella asked if Mrs. Williams was there. He replied that she didn't live there anymore. She was too ill to stay by herself so her family had placed her in McMinnville Nursing Home nearby. He then proceeded to introduce himself. "My name is Evan Camden. My family has lived in McMinnville most all their lives. I am the basketball coach at Warren County High School."

"I lived in McMinnville when I was a little girl and Mrs. Williams' daughter, Maggie, was my best friend," Bella explained. "I have played in this house many times and have a lot of memories here. I found out some time ago when I spoke to Mrs. Williams that Maggie was killed at a young age. I guess I just wanted to relive some things and see how her mom was doing."

"She would probably love to see you if you want to go by the nursing home. She's in room 101," Evan said.

"I'll do that, thank you," Bella returned, reaching out to shake Evan's hand. "Thank you for all the information." She smiled and turned to walk away.

"Hey, if you ever need anything or want more info on how things have changed around here, give me a call. I'm in the book," Evan yelled as her footsteps faded into the distance.

As Bella headed toward home, she decided to take a nostalgic ride around her old hometown. Some things, of course, had changed. Many businesses had closed and new ones had sprung up. New apartment houses were being constructed all over town instead of new houses. At one time this town had been very prosperous and growing in population. Now people were leaving to find work.

Bella didn't want to leave Grandma alone for very long. She had been very depressed about having to sell the farm and leave Maryville. Bella could cheer her up by singing her favorite song, "Be Thou My Vision," which Grandma had found very inspiring.

"Please, Lord," prayed Grandma, "give us that vision you want us to have to know the right thing to do and lead us."

Bella had experienced so much hurt and so many disappointments in her life that she was beginning to wonder if God had forgotten her. She had many prayers to which she could see no answer, and had begun to lose her faith.

"You must always keep the faith." She could hear the echo of Grandma's pleasing voice. "The Lord knows what we need and will provide."

The next day Bella set out looking for employment. She knew that they couldn't survive without it. As she approached the J.C. Penney store downtown, she saw a sign on the window, "Sales Clerks Wanted, No Experience Needed." She gasped and walked in the front door with enthusiasm. The manager was in his office and one of the clerks pointed the way.

Bella knocked on the door and was told to come in. As she sat down in the comfy office chair in front of the manager's desk, he offered her an application and told her to fill it out, and then he would interview her on the spot.

Bella hurriedly gave all the information asked for on the application and handed it back to the manager. He looked it over, asked her some more questions, and told her she was approved for the job.

Immediately, he led her onto the sales floor, introduced her to her co-workers and to the young lady that would be training her. Cindy Gaither — tall, young, and very attractive with a friendly smile — came toward Bella, shook hands and welcomed her to the group.

Bella was so excited to start the new job the next day. She was working the jewelry counter which she dearly loved. Grandma was so thrilled to hear the news. They would be able to survive more abundantly with both incomes.

Thank you, God, for this blessing. Bella did realize she had His help on this one. *But, please, lead my dad home soon. Grandma and I both need him now.*

CHAPTER SIX

Bella and Cindy became very close chums, and Bella was enjoying her job immensely. The manager had agreed to let her work long hours and every day to help with their finances for a while. The other women agreed to give up some of their hours to help out. Bella didn't expect that and was duly grateful for their consideration and sacrifice.

Weeks went by and Grandma became more and more depressed. As a Christian, she knew that God would provide, but her faith was shattered. She just couldn't get back into being herself. Bella tried to help and comfort her as much as possible, but it didn't seem to matter. The singing no longer inspired her; she kept to herself more and more and didn't want to go to church. Bella had made many friends through her job and they would come by to visit Grandma, but to no avail. She drew more into herself and excluded others. Bella knew this was not like Grandma Bailey.

As Bella was making dinner one evening, a knock came on the door. As she opened it, she saw Evan Camden standing there with a big smile on his face and his blue eyes shining.

"Hi, Bella," he said softly. "How are you doing? I just heard your Grandma is ill and I wanted to stop by and see how she is doing."

Evan's presence surprised her. She hadn't heard from him since the day she stopped by Maggie's old house.

"We're doing okay, I guess. Grandma is just very depressed because of all the hurts and disappointments she's gone through the past few years. It's damaging her health and she isn't getting any better. I'm taking her to the doctor tomorrow and see what he says can be done. She's becoming so weak and will hardly get out of bed. I just don't know what to do anymore."

Evan looked at her sadly and told her if he could do anything to let him know. He went through that with his father and knew how she felt.

"Maybe you should just get out of the house for a while. Might make you feel better. How about a dinner and a movie? I hear 'What's Up, Doc?' and 'Diamonds Are Forever' are playing at the Ben Lomand Drive In. They always show two movies on Saturday night. Gillentine's Restaurant is the favorite place for young adults because they have the best pizza in town. Does that sound okay to you?

Bella didn't want to leave Grandma very long but thought it would be good for her to go out for a while. So she agreed to Saturday night around 6:00. It didn't get dark until around 7:00 and that would give them time to have dinner.

Evan arrived at Bella's at 5:45pm and she was ready. She wore her knee-length, yellow, taffeta dress that made her green eyes radiate like emeralds and her red hair glisten. She was a beautiful young woman and Evan was proud to be able to say she was his date.

Bella walked to the car which was a 1971 Trans-Am, red convertible.

As they cruised toward the drive in theater, the conversation was very much with them in mind getting to know each other. He was overly sweet and considerate of her needs, all while watching the movies. At intermission, he went to the concession and bought some popcorn and drinks. Conversation deepened.

After the last movie, it was almost midnight as they left the drive in. On the trip back to Bella's house, she noticed Evan turned onto the wrong road. They were on a dirt lane headed out into the rural area of Warren County.

"Where are we going, Evan?" Bella asked, "You're going too far! Turn around!"

Evan pretended not to hear and kept driving even farther out into the countryside where it was pitch dark and remote. Suddenly, he slammed the car to a halt. Evan moved quickly over to the passenger's side. Bella was a virgin and grew creepily fearful of what Evan had in mind. At that moment, he pounced on top of her and started lifting up her dress. She pushed his hand away with all her gusto, but it was obvious that Evan was the athletic type and powerfully strong. His control was inevitable. His heavy form was covering her, aggressively raping her. She heard herself wailing from the depth of her soul. Her innocence was forever eradicated. She was overwhelmed with pain and guilt. Had she done something wrong? Was all of this really her own fault?

"No, Evan, No!!!!!!" But nothing could change what had been done.

As Evan left her, Bella sat there with her clothes ill arranged and continued to weep.

"Why, Evan? Why did you do this?"

"I knew you were a virgin," he answered very egotistically, "and very lonely since you have moved here. I know I'm very irresistible to young women and I thought I would see if it worked."

"You're a monster. Take me home, please!!" Bella screeched.

"Of course, I got what I wanted," he said, a sheepish grin unmasking his insolence.

Bella remembered what her mother had told her a few years ago about boys. "They only want one thing." Now she thought she might have been right. She had done nothing to provoke this vicious attack.

As soon as she arrived home, Bella ran hurriedly up the steps and through the front door. Luckily for her, Grandma was still in bed.

Where are you dad? she mumbled to herself again. *Why can't you come home? I STILL need you. More than ever!*

CHAPTER SEVEN

Bella awakened to a beautiful, luminous day the next morning with the pain still lingering in her loins and in her heart. She tried in vain to force it out of her mind. After all, she had to take Grandma to see her doctor. She stumbled out of bed, took a shower, and put her jeans and blouse on that she had taken out of her closet the night before. Then she walked across the hallway and woke up Grandma.

"Grandma," she whispered, "it's time to get up and get ready for your doctor's appointment."

Grandma grunted as if to say, "Leave me alone," but she only grunted and stirred. Finally she turned and climbed out of bed. Bella helped her to the shower and laid her clothes out for her to wear. Grandma was still weak and fragile.

They arrived at the doctor's office at 10:00 a.m. and Bella helped Grandma to sit down in the waiting area.

The events of the night before were still lingering in Bella's mind, but she told not a soul for fear someone would think she had provoked it. Grandma was her concern now.

Finally, the nurse called Grandma's name and they entered the exam area. The doctor came into the room shortly and examined Grandma. He looked at Bella and told her he wanted to do some blood tests and an ultrasound of her breasts. He had felt a lump in the left one. Grandma gave her consent and the tests were completed. He said the results would be available shortly if they cared to wait.

After approximately 15 grueling minutes, the doctor walked back into the exam room. His expression was one of sorrow. Bella had seen that expression once before on the face of Dr. Anderson when he gave her the news about Janine's death.

Compassionately, the doctor sat down and took Grandma's and Bella's hands.

"I'm sorry, Mrs. Bailey," he began softly, "but you are in the advanced stages of breast cancer. It would be in your best interest to get your personal affairs in order. I know you want only honesty from me. It seems you only have about 3 months to live, at the most." Dr. Anderson bowed his head and shook it slowly.

Grandma and Bella sat there in astonishment. Their eyes filled with tears and they embraced each other. Bella felt that dagger plunge into her heart again. "We will get her personal affairs together and make some plans.

"Come on, Grandma, let's go home."

Grandma and Bella sat in stunned silence on the ride home. Bella decided she was going to spend as much time as possible with Grandma the next three months. She *really* needed her now.

The next ninety days were very difficult for both Bella and Grandma. Bella saw her countenance fade as she abandoned her will to live. She just lay motionless in her bed all day and night, seldom even rising to eat. Bella brought her meals to the bed, although she seemed she wasn't ingesting enough to keep a bird from swooning.

"Grandma, you have to eat to keep up your strength." Bella's words seemed to slam into a solid shield of resistance.

Grandma's voice was a mere whisper. "Why, I'm going to die anyway. Please just let me go. I want to see my Janine again and the quicker I go, the quicker I'll get to see her."

Bella realized that she didn't want Grandma to suffer any longer. She finally resigned to let her live the rest of her life as she wished.

Although Bella worked the daytime hours, she sat with Grandma during the evenings. Cindy, Bella's friend from work, knew a lady that agreed to stay with Grandma while Bella was working for no charge.

Bella never told anyone about what happened with Evan. Cindy questioned Bella when she came back to work. She wanted to hear all about the date. Bella just told her matter-of-factly that they had gone to dinner and a movie at the drive in theater.

"Evan is just not my type," Bella said. "He is so struck on himself and I don't like men like that. So we agreed not to see each other again." So the subject was conveniently dropped and never dredged up again.

CHAPTER EIGHT

Bella reminisced about Thomas and all the kindness and compassion he had shown to her and Grandma. One morning she decided to give him a call. She knew he would understand her feelings because he really cared about her and she longed to speak openly with a friend — someone who would not adjudicate her.

"Hello." It was Thomas' father who answered.

"Hello, Mr. James? How are you doing? This is Bella Fontaine. Is Thomas at home?"

"Yes, he is, Bella. I'll get him for you."

In just a few seconds, Bella heard Thomas' peaceful voice come on the line. "Bella, is it really you?"

"Yes, it is and I'm so glad to hear your voice," she said with excitement, "How have you been? How is your job at the post office? How is your family?"

"Everything and everybody is great. It's so good to hear your voice also. It is sweet, sweet music to my ears, in fact. How is Grandma doing?" Thomas' tone was reflecting the same jubilance that she was feeling.

Bella couldn't help but amass tears in her eyes. "Grandma isn't doing well at all. The doctor told her last week she has advanced stages of breast cancer and only three months to live. She's only sixty-five years old. That's too young to die. I don't know what I will do without her. She has been my inspiration all my life. I love her with all my heart." Her words cracked and trailed as her heavy sobbing traveled through the phone.

"Oh, I am so sorry, Bella. I know how much you love Grandma and I do, too. How are you dealing with this?" Thomas' voice was laced with sincere compassion.

"I'm okay, but it sure is good to talk to a friend. I was hoping you could come and see me sometime soon. I really need to talk to you," Bella replied, as if begging for a favor. "I can't talk about it any more on the phone."

Thomas thought for a moment. "Ok, I will see what I can do and get there as soon as I can. Is that okay?"

"Yes, of course," Bella replied, calming down somewhat.

As she hung up the receiver, she felt a huge burden lifted off her shoulders just to know Thomas would be there soon. He was a true friend, but somehow she wished it could be more. She realized she had to take care of Grandma now and romance would have to be put off until later. But she cared very deeply for Thomas and hoped the feeling was mutual.

Two weeks passed and she had still heard nothing from Thomas. Then one Wednesday, he called and said he would be coming to visit her that next weekend which was only three days away.

As Bella was preparing for Thomas' visit by cleaning the guest room, she came upon a photo album she had completely forgotten about. As she opened the album, the first few pages were filled with photos of her and her mother together when she was but a little girl. Other pictures were of her father and her together. Friends in McMinnville and Maryville were also in the album. These all brought back bittersweet memories and made Bella feel a little dizzy. She ran to the bathroom where she hung her head over the toilet and was regurgitating for a period of time. "What is wrong with me? I never get sick," she said out loud as if someone could respond. Then she stepped back and it hit her. "What will I do if...?"

The room was clean and fresh the day Thomas arrived. It was a cool, crisp early autumn day in late September, 1971, and the sun was still marching its way through the clouds. This was Bella's favorite time of the year. The Lord's handiwork was in full force and the colors of the trees were becoming amazing. As Bella was staring out the window, hoping to see Thomas, she finally spotted him coming up the walkway and her heart leapt for joy. He was as handsome as ever, but just looked more like a man. She didn't wait for him to arrive at the door, but ran outside and met him with a big hug and kiss.

"What was that?!" Thomas asked with a look of astonishment on his face.

"I am just so thrilled to see you!" Bella answered with happiness in her voice.

They walked arm in arm into the house.

"How are you holding up with your Grandma?" he wanted to know.

Bella sighed. "I guess I am doing as well as expected. She's ready to die and go see my mom. She's waited for this for a long time and doesn't want to put it off any longer. I don't want to see her suffer but I'll truly miss her when she's gone. I won't have anybody left in my family."

Thomas smiled shyly. "You'll have me."

Bella was relieved to hear these soothing words. She just knew he cared about her as much as she cared about him.

Time will tell, she said to herself.

CHAPTER NINE

Thomas had racked up some vacation time at his job, so he decided to take a few days and help Bella take care of Grandma. He would sit with her during the day while Bella worked, and then stay with Bella for a while each night. When sleep would begin to fill his weary eyes, he would drive to the local Americana Motel and rest peacefully, knowing he was doing the right thing. He had deep respect for Bella, and the last thing she needed was for the neighbors to start seedy rumors.

These few days were exceptional to Bella and Thomas because it gave them the opportunity to get to know each other better. But then Thomas had to return to Maryville. She never got enough nerve to tell him about the incident with Evan.

Bella had continually been vomiting in the mornings and decided she would make an appointment with the doctor. It had been two months since Evan had raped her and although she didn't want to think she was pregnant, she couldn't help but suspect the worst.

She called and was surprised to be able to get in the following day. As she drove there, she couldn't help but think about what she would do if she really was going to have a baby. Mixed emotions were jumbled inside of her. She would love to have a baby and be able to give it all the love she had hidden inside of her, but would she be able to support it financially and provide it with all it would need. Abortion was out of the question since she was raised with moral ethics and stringent Christian values.

As she reached Dr. Becket's office, she was trembling with fear, so her hands were shaking. The nurse led her into the examining room and Dr. Becket followed behind.

As the doctor performed the exam, he looked up at Bella and said calmly, "Missy, it looks as if you are about to be a mother. I would say in about seven months. I don't see any reason you shouldn't have a very normal pregnancy. Congratulations!!"

Bella's fears were confirmed, but at the same time she didn't want to be congratulated.

"Congratulations are not in order. I am not married and this baby was conceived through rape," she replied coldly, "You don't understand. I don't know what I will do. A baby doesn't fit into my plans for my life. I NEVER want the father to even know about his baby. He is a jerk!! Please doctor, don't tell anyone."

Dr. Becket assured Bella that he was not permitted to tell anyone without her consent because of the "patient-doctor confidentiality" laws. This reassured her and she knew she could keep it quiet for a while. But Bella knew people would eventually know when her belly started to grow.

So now I have to make some important decisions for myself and my baby, she thought.

Bella was steaming with anger toward Evan. She wanted to vent these feelings but didn't have anyone she could talk to. So she turned to God. "Please, God, take away this anger I have for Evan so I can give this baby all the love it needs while I am carrying it in my body. Help me to make the right decision about its life and what would be best for the baby." Bella would pray this prayer every day while she was pregnant.

Grandma continually grew worse and was now sleeping the majority of the time. One night, as Bella was preparing for bed, she decided to go into Grandma's room and check on her. As she entered the room, Grandma stirred in her bed and asked Bella to come close.

"Bella, dear," Grandma said softly, "you have had a very hard life with many trials and disappointments. You have had to take on more responsibility before most children your age. Through all this, I feel your faith is not as strong as it should be.

"Bella, don't give up on God. He has much in store for your life but you don't realize it yet. He has given you the gift of a child. That is the most precious gift He can give you."

Bella looked at Grandma in astonishment. "How did you know? Did Dr. Becket call you?"

"No, he didn't. You know you can't keep anything from me. I know you better than you know yourself. You have been sick and I recognize the symptoms. Just take care of yourself and this baby while you're pregnant and if you feel you can't keep it, give it up for adoption to a Christian family that can love and support it and raise it to be a fine man or woman. They would be able to give it what it needs spiritually and financially. "

Bella had tears in her eyes by now and responded softly. "But, Grandma, there is something you don't know about this pregnancy. Evan forced himself on me that night! I was a virgin and he took advantage of me! Then he just laughed about it and said he just wanted to prove he could take me." She couldn't keep from showing anger in her voice.

Grandma didn't seem to be surprised. "I know you are not the type of girl to "sleep around" and I knew something of that nature had to have happened. Evan is the one to ask God for forgiveness. You didn't do anything wrong. Forgive yourself, Bella, and go on with your life."

Grandma continued after resting for a moment, "Pursue your education and be the fine nurse you want to be. Don't give up on finding your father. God will lead you to him some day when it is the right time."

By this time, Bella was sobbing.

"Oh, Grandma, you have always guided me in the right direction and I trust you now. I will take your advice and do as you say."

As soon as Bella had finished speaking, Grandma gazed into the distance and gasped with a smile, "Janine, is that you? Have you come to take me home? I am ready to go!" With those loving words on her lips, she closed her eyes and drew her final breath.

Bella had tried to prepare herself for this dreadful moment, but the emptiness still seemed more than she could bear. She broke down and cried hysterically. Grandma was just like a mother to her and now she had lost both of them.

"Oh, Grandma," Bella cried, "please don't go. I need you more than ever now!"

Grandma had wanted to die at home instead of in a hospital. Bella felt so truly alone now.

She sat with Grandma for a little while before she called the doctor to come and pronounce her dead and fill out the death certificate. After that, the doctor proceeded to call the local funeral home to come for the body. Grandma would be sent back to Maryville for the final funeral arrangements since all of Grandma's and Grandpa's friends and family were there. She would later be laid to rest next to Grandpa and Janine.

The next day, Bella phoned all the local friends, her manager at J.C. Penney, Cindy, Kathy, and Thomas. She wanted to speak with them personally. They gave her their sympathies and said they would be at the funeral.

Bella arrived in Maryville and went to the funeral home which Grandma had previously chosen. She had made the arrangements a few years before, so the director knew her wishes better than anyone.

The funeral was held on a cool, gloomy, rainy day in late autumn. The chapel was full of family and friends and Bella was met with many hugs and sympathies. She was introduced to a number of people that had known Grandma in school when they were children. She was still fairly young and many of her classmates were still living.

Bella's heart sank and part of her being went into that ground with Grandma. She was so confused as to what she should do concerning Grandma's advice. Where should she start? What should she do first? How can she keep this secret?

Bella thought again, *Dad, where are you? I am so alone now and need you so much!! Please come back!*

On the day after the funeral, Bella was contacted by Grandma's attorney in downtown Maryville. She was told that Grandma had a last will and testament and he wanted her to make an appointment to come into his office to present this to her. Since she was staying in

Maryville with Kathy's parents, she set it for the *following day.*

As Bella walked into the attorney's office, the receptionist greeted her with a smile, "Hello. May I help you?" she said.

Bella returned the smile.

"I'm here to see Mr. Stanford."

The receptionist led Bella to his office and opened the door where Bella could see the attorney sitting behind a large, dark mahogany desk. He rose from his seat and offered Bella his hand in an introduction.

"Hi, Miss Fontaine. Please have a seat and we will proceed to get down to business."

After she was seated, Attorney Stanford proceeded.

"As you know Mrs. Bailey did not have many possessions after the sale of her farm, but what she did have, she wanted you to inherit. First, she was able to purchase her horse, Molly, back from the man who bought the farm when Molly got too old for the children to ride. As you know, she is staying at the McCormick farm. They have agreed to provide for her the rest of her days."

Bella was thrilled, and her eyes were filled with tears.

"Also, all her antique furniture," Stanford continued, "and $20,000 your Grandma had remaining after she paid the mortgage balance on the farm. It is yours. Use it wisely."

Bella was astonished. "Oh, Grandma, thank you so much," she said under her breath. She knew Grandma could hear her. "Thank you for everything."

The following day, Bella returned to McMinnville and the loneliness of the home she had made with Grandma.

I have nobody here now, she thought. *My friends have their lives and my life should be in Maryville where I grew up. I know they will understand.*

CHAPTER TEN

As Bella's introspection returned to 2010, she prepared herself for the tour she had planned on Easter Island. All the sites could be visited without charge and were located primarily along the enchanting Pacific coastline.

Two exceptional points of interest were the volcanic craters of Rano Kau and Rano Raraku, the latter being where the moai carvings were born. Hundreds of laborers carved full time to form them out of the hillside of volcanic rock.

Rano Kau, the remains of a volcanic cinder cone, is filled with fresh rainwater and has a mottled unearthly appearance that is breathtaking.

Bella soaked in the aura of the white sand beaches, Anakina and Ovahe.

She discovered a large number of quaint shops geared toward tourists as well as an open market. Vendors of the same type souvenirs were hawking their wares at each site—mostly moai-inspired trinkets.

Bella was not disappointed in her time expended on Easter Island. The remoteness of the locale created a relaxing calm for which she had hungered a long time. The beauty she experienced was matchless in her memories, and being able to view the eclipse was a dream come true.

As she returned to her room at the guest house, located in town, she decided to rest for the remainder of the evening. The hour was late, so she fixed a sandwich for dinner and sat up in bed for a while, recalling the uniqueness of the day.

While sitting there etching notes in her journal, her thoughts reverted to the past and her heart leapt as she remembered the feelings she had experienced while pregnant with her child and the plans she had to make immediately.

After much inward debate, Bella made the firm decision to move back to Maryville. Her friends were there and in McMinnville she was alone. So the following day, she called a van company and scheduled the move for the next week. She contacted her manager at J.C.

Penney, Cindy and her landlord. After telling them the situation, they were very understanding. She only gave one week's notice because she knew that soon the evidence of her pregnancy would be showing. Cindy agreed to keep in touch.

That week passed quickly and Bella worked her normal hours at the department store and packed her belongings at night. She hardly had time to rest and it was taking a toll on her. When she phoned Thomas, he gladly offered to come and help. She didn't know what she would do without him sometimes. He was like a true blood brother.

The McCormicks asked Bella to stay with them until she could find a place of her own. After stuffing her furniture in a rented storage bin, she hauled her personal belongings to their house. Kathy was still away at college in South Carolina and it gave them comfort to have a girl around the house during that time. Kathy was home on weekends and Bella relished having her there for companionship.

Even though Bella had the pregnancy to be concerned about, she enrolled in the College of Nursing at the University of Tennessee in Knoxville the following week. She would have to wait until the next semester to start, but she didn't mind. Grandma wanted her to pursue her education and she felt she shouldn't wait any longer than absolutely necessary.

Bella understood there would be many rumors and talk behind her back about the pregnancy but she was prepared for that and thought she could handle the situation. After all, she wouldn't be the only pregnant woman at the university. Everyone believed that the baby's father had been killed in a car accident and she was sticking to that story. She was not emotionally stable enough to handle everyone knowing about the rape. *Maybe,* she thought, *I will receive sympathy instead of ridicule and judgment.*

This event marked the beginning of many substantial changes in Bella's life and she was not prepared for what was about to happen.

CHAPTER ELEVEN

In January 1972, Bella began the semester at the College of Nursing at the University of Tennessee Knoxville. The College of Nursing was established in July 1971 in response to a long-recognized and well-established need for nurses prepared at the collegiate level.

The University was displaying their commitment to advancing the mission to educate nurses to meet the challenges of an ever-changing healthcare system.

The Vision Statement of the University states that it intends to be the preeminent public research and teaching facility linking the people of Tennessee to the nation and the world.

Bella was able to acquire an apartment on campus and a job at the campus bookstore. Her life was looking up and all things were positive. She loved her life now and even looked forward to the birth of her baby.

Everyone Bella met in Knoxville was very friendly and kind to her and not judgmental of her pregnancy. She made friends easily with the local people and the campus was very much crime-free. Security was unusually tight on campus, so she felt comfortable walking back and forth between the bookstore and her apartment at night. *Life is really good*, she thought.

The next few months of her pregnancy went by quickly since she was able to stay busy with school and her job.

One night, after she arrived home from the bookstore, she began having contractions. They were still one hour apart, so she didn't get too excited, thinking they were probably just false labor. Then, toward morning, they became more stringent and closer together. She called the ambulance service at Baptist Hospital where her mother had been employed earlier. By the time she arrived at the hospital, her water had broken. The nurses would not let her raise up from the gurney and rushed her into the labor room. As she lay there, the doctor came in and examined her. He told her she was in stage two dilation and that she must relax. As time passed, the contractions became worse. In approximately four hours, she was taken into the delivery room. The nurses proceeded to tell her it was time for the baby to come. It seemed as if it went quickly and Bella could hear the cry of her newborn.

Her heart jumped for joy, then the nurse handed the baby to her and for the first time, she held him (yes, a boy) in her arms. She had never felt that kind of love before. It overwhelmed her!

"I am a mother," she whispered to the nurse.

"Yes, you are, dear, and you have a very healthy baby boy," the nurse smiled. "God has truly blessed you."

But Bella knew what she must do. Her jubilance quickly diminished. The nurse took the baby when she was rolled into her room. She knew that she would not be able to see him again. The hospital, of course, had been informed of her adoption wishes.

Bella cried into her pillow all night. In two days, the adoption agency came and took her baby boy away. They had found a caring Christian family with whom to place him, and they had told Bella about their choice. She was pleased and knew he would be well taken care of. The name of the family was not disclosed to Bella and she was not able to see her baby boy again. But inside her, there was a new hunger.

Bella was soon able to return to her nursing studies and her fellow students and friends knew her request. Respectfully, they didn't ask any questions about the child. Classes went on as if nothing had happened. Bella attended parties and everyone tried to fill her time with activities but it would not fill the hole left by the taking away of her baby. She would always love him and wonder where he was every day, all her life.

Bella attended college full time, even going to classes during the summer break. Finally, in 1974, she was granted her nursing degree, graduating with honors. She was offered employment at Baptist Hospital in the

Pediatrics Nursing Department. She couldn't have been more thrilled! Her love for babies was obvious; and maybe, this could help fill the hollowness in her heart for her son.

Over the next several months, she toiled many long hours, working every day she could in order to be close to the babies. She felt she was an excellent nurse and had a calming effect on the little ones. The staff loved Bella and knew she was a kind and loving individual. They all were aware that she had given up her son for adoption and could feel her anguish.

After working a long shift with ten babies to attend to in the hospital nursery, she felt the craving for a break. She took the lengthy walk to the elevator and down to the cafeteria on the second floor, where she purchased a hot cup of coffee and a Danish pastry. While sitting and resting, a tall, dark, handsome man strolled up to her and spoke.

"Mind if I sit with you for a while?"

Bella looked up and came into eye contact with this striking gentleman.

"No, not at all. Sit down."

He had a very kind, gentle smile and pleasing attitude. As they parlayed, she found out that he was the son of Dr. Anderson—the doctor who performed the surgery on her mom. His name was Dr. Brent Nathan Anderson. He, also, was a doctor of Internal Medicine. Bella was so proud to meet him and told him how much she appreciated his dad doing what he could for her mother.

Dr. Brent Anderson also knew the situation she had endured with her son but did not mention that to Bella at this time. He was thoughtful enough to know it would hurt too much for her to talk about it. So they just sat for a while and got acquainted with each other. They talked mostly about the hospital and how much they enjoyed working there.

After about 30 minutes, he rose from his seat.

"If you will excuse me," he said, "I have to get back to work. Enjoy the rest of your day. We are lucky to have you working here. Take care." His soft eyes were smiling. "I hope to see you again."

After he left, Bella felt in her heart that she would see him again soon and get a chance to know him better.

The weeks elapsed and Bella merely continued her mundane routine—go to work, work twelve hours a day, then go home, eat, watch TV, then flop into bed.

It had been a while since they had talked, so one night she decided to call Kathy, who was now out of college, and living in Maryville with her parents. She was employed as an attorney working with abused children. Kathy told her that she had met a man while in college who was now living in Knoxville, working as a Court Judge. They had fallen in love and were engaged to be married. Bella was thrilled.

"Oh, Kathy, I am so happy for you. What's his name? When is the big day?"

"We haven't set a date yet," Kathy replied, "but it will probably be within the next few months. Oh, Bella, he's such a great Christian man and I love him so much and he loves me.

His name is Robert Hardcastle, Judge Robert Hardcastle."

As Bella was talking to Kathy, her mind wandered to Thomas, whom she also hadn't heard from in quite a while.

"Kathy, do you know anything about Thomas," Bella asked.

Kathy hesitated. "Didn't you hear?" she said sadly, "He was drafted and went to Vietnam a few months ago."

"Oh, Kathy, I hope he comes home soon."

Her thoughts ran to the news she had seen on TV about the fierce fighting going on in the war. Quickly she changed the subject back to the wedding.

"Kathy, please let me know when you set the date for the wedding. Robert sounds like a great guy and you deserve the best."

"Of course I will, since I want you to be my Maid of Honor. Will you do that for me?" Kathy replied with joy in her voice.

"Of course *I* will," Bella repeated with bubbly excitement.

Bella had previously informed Kathy of the birth of her baby boy. Since Kathy was her best friend, she had heartfelt sympathy for Bella but understood her decision. She knew Bella was a strong woman and would make it through anything life could throw at her. She would survive—one day at a time.

CHAPTER TWELVE

As Bella hung up the phone, the devastating news about Thomas seemed to flood through her being and wash away whatever faith she may have held on to. Yet prayer was the only straw of hope which she knew to grasp.

"*Oh, God,*" Bella prayed, *you have to let him come back to us.*" She had just begun to realize how deep her feelings ran for this phantom friend.

A few weeks ran by before Kathy called. "Bella," she said, excitement exploding in her voice, "we have finally set the date for the wedding. It's June 9th. Oh, Bella," she continued without hesitating, "you're still going to be able to be my Maid of Honor, aren't you? The wedding is going to be magnificent! My dress is gorgeous and yours will be, too. We're going to have it at Robert's parents' home, which is a beautiful Victorian, three-story house in the countryside outside of Maryville. Well, really it's near Walland. Surrounding the house is a picturesque garden filled with many brilliantly colored roses. It's totally awesome! They employ a group of gardeners who care for the lawn and flower garden to the nth degree. You just can't imagine! You'll just have to see it for yourself." Kathy went on and on with Bella wondering if she was ever going to reach a slow-down point.

Kathy seemed to take a breath, and then continued. "On the back lawn, at the end of a long walkway, there's a gazebo, which is where the ceremony will be held. It's perfect!"

"Whoa, whoa, slow down, Kathy!" Bella interrupted. You sold me! It sounds great and I'm so happy for you. Yes, I already promised you I will be proud to be your Maid of Honor."

"Oh, Bella," Kathy said, "Robert and I are going to be so happy together. I really feel we are soul mates and God has brought us together. Thank the Lord!"

"You will need to come to Maryville and be fitted for your dress. When can you come?" Kathy asked.

"Will next weekend be okay?"

"That will be great! I look forward to seeing you again." Kathy sighed as she hung up the phone.

Bella was really tired when she finished talking with Kathy and retired to bed for the night. It was getting late and she had to get up early for work in the morning, but she couldn't keep from wondering when the day was going to come when she would meet *her* soul mate. She could hear in her mind Grandma saying, *In God's own time, Bella dear. Be patient.*

CHAPTER THIRTEEN

As Bella returned to the hospital to work the next day, she was met by several nurses asking about problems that had occurred over the weekend. Her position was very stressful — dealing with employees, patients, doctors, and co-workers.

While attempting to delve into these problems, she came face-to-face with Brent in the hallway on his way to visit a patient.

"Hello, again," he smiled.

Bella's heart skipped a beat as she almost ran into him. "Yes, hello, again," she returned. *Can't I think of anything else to say?*

"You know, Bella," he began, "I was wondering if you would do me the honor of having dinner with me Saturday night?"

"Well," Bella looked stunned but elated, "yes, I'd be happy to."

"Could I pick you up around 7:00?" Brent asked with glee. "Do you like Italian?"

"Yes, and I love it," she said, answering both questions at once.

"OK, 7:00 o'clock it is. See you then," he said as he walked away and continued to see his patient.

Saturday night came quickly and Brent was right on time. The doorbell rang at Bella's small apartment and as she opened the door, there he stood, looking striking, holding a lovely bouquet of seasonal flowers, which he preceded to place in her hand.

"Thank you so much," she smiled. "They're beautiful. Please come in while I find a vase to put these in some water."

Brent stepped inside and eyed the apartment Bella had leased when she came to Knoxville. It was an efficiency apartment but was perfect for her. She was not at home much and didn't have a lot of furniture. It was also very economical with low utilities. Although she did bring some of Grandma's antiques with her, she had to put some in storage, feeling that some day she may have a home of her own.

After she placed the flowers in a vase, they left for the reservation at the nicest Italian restaurant in Knoxville. As they walked in the door, the hostess said their table was ready. Brent was very well known in town and treated with utmost dignity.

As they were seated, the waiter handed the menu to Brent and he ordered for both of them.

"I hope you don't mind, Bella," he said. "I know what food is best here and I'm sure you won't be disappointed."

"No, of course not," she answered, glad he ordered for her because she didn't have a clue what most of the food on the menu even was.

Brent was charming, well-mannered, and sincerely considerate of Bella's feelings that night. He showed her nothing but respect. As she listened to his conversing, she drank in every word. They chatted for hours and felt as if they had known each other all their lives.

When the dinner was over, Brent drove Bella home and said goodnight at the door.

"I hope you had a nice time." A sparkle was in his handsome eyes.

"Oh, it was wonderful!" she replied, hoping he would ask her out again.

"May I see you again?" he was smiling. "I hope you know what I mean. We'll see each other at the hospital, but I want to see you again for a date."

"I would love that," she said. "Just call me."

With that said, he turned and walked away.

Bella was so thrilled. Brent was such a nice guy and she knew they were very compatible. Before she fell asleep that night, a lovely thought skipped through her mind, *Grandma, maybe this is the one.*

Bella and Brent began to become a pair. They made a lunch date every day and just sat and talked. One day while eating lunch, Brent asked Bella if she would go with him on his family cabin cruiser on Watts Bar Lake located between Knoxville and Chattanooga on the Tennessee River.

The trip was set for the next Saturday and they spent all day on the cruiser. The weather was picturesque—a sunny, brisk day. The waters were calm and supremely relaxing. Brent and Bella needed a stress-free day. A picnic lunch had been prepared by Bella. Brent was a great navigator and they just took a slow pace, cherishing their time together.

As the sun began to set and the dusk fall, the glow on the horizon was magnificent. The sky had stripes of delightful variant hues of orange, yellow, and red. God's handiwork was obvious that night. Later, they lay awake on the deck of the cruiser gazing up at the dark sky locating and naming the constellations. Brent was extremely knowledgeable about astrology. All at once, they saw a shooting star glaze the sky. Startled, they looked at each other while making wishes under their breath. Time would tell if their wishes came true.

As the hour was getting late, Bella turned to Brent, "I think it is time for me to go home."

"Oh, do we have to, Bella? I have enjoyed this day tremendously. Haven't you?" Brent anticipated an answer but knew what she would say.

"Yes, I have very much," she replied with rapture in her voice. "Please, let's do it again soon before the weather gets too cold."

"We'll do that," said Brent.

As they took the cruiser back to the marina and walked to the car, Brent put his arm around Bella's shoulder and pulled her close to him. As their eyes collided, he kissed her gently. Bella passionately returned the motion of the feeling which seemed to consume her.

Brent looked at her with his soft brown eyes.

"Bella," he said, "I think I'm falling in love with you."

Bella didn't know how to respond. She had never felt this way before about a man, except her father, of course, but that was certainly different.

Bella was quiet all the way home from the marina. Brent didn't know how to interpret her silence.

When they arrived at Bella's apartment and Brent walked her to the door, she turned to him, breaking her reticence.

"I think I am falling in love with you, too, Brent. It's just that I haven't felt this way before and it's new to me. Please forgive me for not saying so sooner. There are things in my past I have had to deal with for the last few years. There will come a time that I will explain them to you."

With that said, they kissed one more time then said goodnight.

Needless to say, Bella hardly slept all night thinking about what Brent told her. *Please, God, she prayed, let him be the one.*

CHAPTER FOURTEEN

Father Time seemed to have sprouted wings.

It was already May and the date for Kathy's wedding was drawing near. Bella had gone to Maryville a few weeks earlier to be fitted for her dress. Kathy was right when she said it was "gorgeous." It was floor-length with a deep neckline and slim bodice. And it was peach, Bella's favorite color. With her red hair, Bella exemplified "stunning."

Kathy had asked several of her friends to be her Bridesmaids. Their dresses were tailored the same, but were in yellow instead of peach.

The week before the wedding, Bella decided to ask Brent to attend the event with her. She thought it was time to let Kathy know about their relationship. Brent was thrilled to go. He was anxious to become acquainted with Bella's friends.

Bella and Brent drove to Maryville early the day of the wedding to help with the arrangements. Kathy was, to say the least, a bundle of nerves.

Robert and his parents greeted them and asked Bella to try to help Kathy gain her composure.

"I know this is the right thing because Robert and I love each other very much and want to spend the rest of our lives together, but I'm so nervous!" Kathy said, her hands shaking.

"Kathy," Bella reassured her, "everyone is nervous on their wedding day. That's only natural."

Kathy thanked Bella for coming early and giving her the encouragement she needed.

All the decorations were in place. Yellow and peach roses cascaded along the porch railings for the entire length. Beside the walkway, streamers of peach and yellow were lining the padded folding chairs that were sitting in rows for the guests. The gazebo was decorated with beautiful arrangements of roses in varying shades of peach and yellow.

As the ceremony got underway, the Maid of Honor, along with the Bridesmaids, began strolling down the aisle of the walkway, stepping to the beat of the music.

The guests rose from their seats as Kathy materialized from the darkness. Bella could detect the gasps of awe from the at least 100 guests when Kathy started her march as the bride. Kathy was breathtaking as her dress flowed from her body in trains of silk. Her veil cloaked her face and hung long in the back past her waist. Her bouquet was fashioned of yellow and peach roses tumbling in a trail from her hands along with streamers of matching colors.

The smile on her face was brilliantly radiant. As she approached Robert, he reached out and grasped her hand. The love in their eyes was glowing, flooding their faces with radiance.

The pastor began the ceremony vows and the service was completed in barely twenty minutes. He then pronounced them Mr. and Mrs. Robert Hardcastle.

As the charming couple marched down the aisle for the first time as husband and wife, the guests cheered in accelerating applause.

Brent met Bella at the front porch and entered the house for the reception. They were immediately greeted warmly by Kathy, Robert, and their parents.

Tables were lined up with mountains of luscious food served by a top-notch catering company. Bella had never seen such a vast display of cuisine! Centerpieces on each table were made from roses using the same color scheme as the wedding.

At the reception, Bella introduced Brent to Kathy and Robert. He was asked to sit at the table with the wedding party where he could become acquainted with Bella's friends.

Brent was welcomed by everyone and liked by all.

Bella was so proud of him and his accomplishments in life. She knew they loved each other and, just like Robert and Kathy, wanted to spend the rest of their lives together.

Shortly after the reception, Brent asked Bella to go outside where they could be alone. He then removed a small box from his jacket pocket. Since it looked like a box that might contain a ring, Bella gasped with excitement.

"Oh, Brent, you didn't!" she said, clasping her hand over her mouth.

"Oh, yes, I did," remarked Brent, while he bent down to the ground on one knee.

"Bella Fontaine, will you marry me?" he asked with enthusiasm. "Will you be my wife forever?"

Bella extended her hand as Brent slid the ring onto her finger. It was at least a two carat round-shaped diamond solitaire. As he rose to stand, she jumped into his arms.

"Yes, yes, yes! I will marry you and be your wife forever!"

They kissed for what seemed several minutes then agreed to wait until the wedding reception was over to inform Kathy and Robert of their engagement.

As they wandered back into the house, Kathy could see the light in their eyes.

"What happened while you two were outside?" she asked, with a smirk-like look on her face.

"Oh, we don't want to take the attention from your special day. It can wait," Bella said, grinning from ear to ear.

"Come on, Bella," Kathy said, "you're my best friend. You can tell me anything."

"Well," Bella began, "Brent asked me to marry him. Look at this gorgeous ring! I said 'Yes', of course!"

"Oh, Bella, I'm so delighted for both of you. I know you'll be very happy together. You were made for each other. And by the way, the ring is GORGEOUS!!" Kathy yipped with excitement, jumping up and down on her tiptoes.

Robert and Kathy left for their honeymoon in Hawaii and Brent and Bella returned to Knoxville. On the drive back home, they set their wedding date for September 10th. The day had been so long and full of excitement, they both agreed they'd have trouble sleeping that night, but looked forward to planning their future together.

CHAPTER FIFTEEN

As Bella stood at the window of her suite the next morning in Easter Island having her first cup of coffee, her thoughts flashed to the real purpose of her trip. Of course she came to see the eclipse, but she had also made the commitment to travel to Santiago, Chile to investigate the devastation caused by the earthquake that hit there five months before, on February 27th. The need for medical aid to the people had haunted her conscience ever since that day, and she made a vow to God to serve wherever she was needed. Because of her haunting past, she felt drawn to this mission.

The magnitude of the quake was 8.8 for only the duration of 90 seconds. Many cities in Chile, including Santiago, were devastated. Cities experiencing the strongest shaking were Arauco and Coronel. Others were Concepcion, Valparaiso, and Talca.

The earthquake triggered a tsunami which damaged several coastal towns in south central Chile and also the port of Talcahuano. A blackout was generated that affected 93% of the population and went for several days. The latest death toll as of May 15, 2010 was 521 victims — earlier suspected to be over 800.

It was estimated that the quake was so powerful it may have shortened the length of the day by 1.26 microseconds and moved the Earth's figure axes by 8 cm.

The day after the earthquake, curfews were imposed in some cities due to looting and public disorder. Special Forces were called in, but to no avail. The looting and pillaging continued.

Two million people were affected by the quake with more than 500,000 homes completely demolished in many cities. People were sleeping in tents and on the streets for fear of going into the buildings.

A travel alert was issued and it was for this reason that Bella did not attempt to go there until this time. She was able to go by plane to Santiago, then by bus to the other cities.

Santiago's health minister estimated the cost of rebuilding hospitals destroyed at some $3.6

billion. The work of reconstruction, Alvaro Erazo said, would take at least three years, adding that during this period, hospitals will be installed in the affected areas of central and southern Chile.

The United Nations Secretary, General Ban Ki-Moon, while visiting Santiago, promised quick aid deliveries to President Michelle Bachelet and President-Elect Sebastian Pinera. The U.N. spokesperson had stated that Chile would need temporary bridges, field hospitals, satellite phones, electricity, generators, damage assessment teams, water purification systems, field kitchens, and dialysis centers.

As Bella entered the city of Santiago, she could see people sleeping in tents in the streets. Hunger was rampant; food contamination was everywhere; water was not drinkable; medical personnel were rushing to and fro trying to treat the sick and injured in field hospitals set up in the streets. She truly could discern the vital need for aid in many different fields of expertise. It seemed that aid couldn't get there fast enough. People were still dying.

Bella's heart went out to the victims and also to the people trying to bring the aid. She decided she had to do what she could with her skills and abilities to serve those people.

With this experience in her heart and mind, she returned to Easter Island after the long, grueling day to get some rest. The following day she would contact the necessary authorities about going back to Chile to offer her services.

Why do things like this have to happen, Lord? What is the reason? What position am I to serve in your will?

Please help these people of Chile, she prayed, *and bless them with the aid they need. Give me the strength to do your will and your purpose in my life. Stop the dying and suffering, please! Amen.*

CHAPTER SIXTEEN

Needless to say, Bella was unable to sleep a wink that night, and her mind flashed back to her life with Brent.

Bella and Brent returned to work the next day after Kathy's ceremony, and the hospital was buzzing with the news of *their* upcoming wedding. All the female employees were gazing in awe at the enormous ring on Bella's left hand. She was ecstatic and bubbling over!

"Man, what a rock!" said Nurse Brown. "He must love you a lot. That is really exquisite!"

Time went by quickly between June and September and many arrangements had to be agreed upon. The wedding was to take place at Brent's parent's home outside Knoxville in the Farragut community. It was an upscale neighborhood where many of the local doctors and lawyers resided.

The guest list was much larger than that of Kathy and Robert. It was filled with physicians and medical professionals they both knew at the hospital and with whom they had been co-workers for quite some time. Brent had many family members that would be arriving from all over the state of Tennessee, but Bella had no family. She found herself wishing her dad could be there to give her away, but she would have to walk down the aisle alone.

September 10 was a very sunny, cool, crisp day but the autumn hues of browns, golds, and reds had not yet started showing their colors.

Kathy and Robert showed up the night before the wedding to help with the arrangements. The Andersons were very kind and made certain the "best" was prepared; the "best" caterer; "best" entertainment; "best" florist; "best" decorations.

Everything went off without a hitch. The guests were all on time and the service started precisely as planned.

Bella's dress was a long, formal length white satin with a fitted waist and bodice. It had a plunging neckline. At the back, secured in the middle of her waist, was a long train that hung to the floor. Her veil was full and hung down her back to her waist. The Bridesmaids and Kathy wore red dresses, tailored similar to Bella's. Red and whites roses were the colors of choice.

Bella and Brent had written their own vows which were full of love and commitment for each other. Their faces glowed with the radiance that captivated their hearts.

After the charming ceremony in the colossal family room, the reception was held in the grand dining area. Like Kathy's, it was most expertly catered. There was everything from hors devours to escargot. There also were exquisite sandwiches cut in wedges, roast duckling and sautéed shrimp. Whatever the pallets of the guests could crave, the caterers had assembled. The entertainment was a small orchestra of professionals who had performed all over the world. When the music started, Bella and Brent had the first dance celebrating the rest of their lives.

Please, Lord, don't let this ever end. This is the happiest moment of my life, Bella prayed.

She peered up at Brent, her sparkling eyes full of sentiment. "I love you," she whispered, "with all my heart."

"I love you, too," Brent responded, "and will love you always."

Las Vegas was the city they had chosen for their honeymoon because of the excitement and adventure.

Bella had never traveled much, and to go to a place even similar to Las Vegas was a dream come true.

Bella and Brent decided to live in his apartment in downtown Knoxville. It was convenient to the hospital and made it easy to commute when they were both on call. Even though it was small and Bella had to put most of her possessions from her apartment in storage with the rest of her furniture, she thought it best until they decided to start a family.

Bella's life with Brent was filled with more love and excitement than she had ever dreamed life could be. Every day was a new day and every moment a new happening. She felt as if she was living a dream of some fairy princess. Brent was the best husband any woman could ask for. His kindness and generosity left her in awe. She had never been treated so well.

Five years passed quickly, and the marriage had its ups and downs, as most marriages do, but they never stopped loving each other. When it was time to start a family, they decided to both make an appointment with Dr. Stanley, a fertility specialist in Knoxville. After the necessary tests were performed, it was found that Bella had a problem.

"One of your tests showed an abnormality, Bella, and I would like you to go to the hospital tomorrow morning for a uterine biopsy," Dr. Stanley remarked, with concern in his voice.

Since Bella was a nurse, she could envision the possibilities.

"Oh, no! Does that mean it could be cancer?"

"I'm not sure. Let's pray for the best and not think the worst, okay?"

Brent and Bella were silent on the drive home. Bella had agreed to have the biopsy the next morning. It would be a couple of days before she would know the results—a very anxious two days.

When the results were in, Dr. Stanley phoned Bella and gave her the news.

"Bella, I am afraid I have bad news. You DO have uterine cancer. But there's good news, too. We have caught it in time. You will, of course, have to undergo chemotherapy treatments. We need to start as soon as possible," Dr. Stanley replied with sadness yet urgency in his tone.

Bella just stood there in shock, holding the phone.

Why me, Lord? Why now? We have been so happy. What is Brent going to think? Will our marriage be able to survive this crisis?

"Of course, Dr. Stanley," Bella said, "whatever I need to do. Let's just get this started as quickly as possible. My grandmother had cancer and I know what I'll have to go through."

After Bella hung up, she heard Brent enter the front door.

"I'm home, Bella, where are you?"

"Here I am," Bella said, as she entered the room. "I have some bad news, Brent. Dr. Stanley just called and gave me the results of my biopsy. It wasn't good. I have uterine cancer," she said as she began to sob heavily. "I have to start chemo as soon as possible."

Brent reached out and took her into his arms to comfort her but also felt an emptiness inside. He knew that meant the chemo would prevent her from any pregnancy. His heart sank at the thought of never being a dad. That was a dream he and Bella both had—to be able to have children.

As the sun rose in its magnificence, a dark cloud hung over Bella and Brent when they entered the hospital and walked down the hallway to the exam room for the chemo. Brent stood by Bella's side as the procedure was performed and she felt comfort from his spirit running through her body. He could feel her pain and sorrow.

Several months went by and Bella went through the necessary chemo treatments. She remained in the apartment and fell into a state of depression. Brent decided to hire an LPN to stay with her full time.

As Bella became more and more depressed, she took more and more medication. It wasn't long before her personality changed. She became easily agitated and lost her temper. Brent couldn't keep a nurse employed because Bella would become very distressed about insignificant situations and fly into a rage.

Brent began working long hours at the hospital and after several weeks, a rumor was running rampant through the premises that he was having an affair with a nurse named Jennifer Smith. She was an undeniably pretty woman with blonde hair hanging to her shoulders, blue eyes and a trim figure. She and Brent had been co-workers for many years. A short time ago, Jennifer lost her husband to cancer and could understand the feelings Brent had about Bella going through this ordeal. Compassion and understanding helped them comfort each other and they began growing closer. Bella could understand how this easily could have led to an affair.

One evening when Brent returned home late, Bella was waiting up for him.

"Brent," she began, "are you having an affair with Jennifer Smith?"

Brent was taken by surprise and stuttered "B-- Bella, what are you talking about?"

"There have been rumors at the hospital that this is true and has been going on for a while," she said with anger in her eyes.

"Oh, Bella, it wasn't supposed to happen like this," Brent stammered, "I've been so lonely without you. We hardly see each other since your sickness. You're taking more and more pills and it's altering your personality. I can't stand to be around you anymore! This crisis has broken my heart and I just couldn't deal with it. Yes, it is true. Jennifer and I are in love with each other. I will always love you, Bella, but I also love her. I'm asking you for a divorce. You can't have children and being a dad is very important to me. Jennifer is pregnant and I really want to be a dad to her baby. I'm so sorry, Bella, that it happened this way. Please forgive me."

Brent flopped down on the couch, hid his face in his hands and began to cry.

Bella didn't know what to say. She had felt in her heart that it was true. The love she had for him had not subsided, and she was devastated and angry.

"Forgive you, of course. I know you loved me at one time and I know you always wanted to be a dad. This is something that neither one of us could control. The depression and pills are all my fault. Nobody can cope with being around me. I can't cope with this myself! Believe me, I understand, but I don't like it. If you file for divorce, I won't give you a fight. But one thing, I don't want any alimony. You are no longer obligated to me. Your new family should be your priority now."

Brent had already moved to their bedroom and silently begun packing a small suitcase of his belongings.

After he left, Bella broke down in tears.

Oh, God, what do I do now? I just don't know if I can go on living. That would be wrong and out of your will, but this pain is more than I can bear.

She took more pills and went to bed.

In barely a week, Bella received the divorce papers, signed "on the dotted line" and returned them to Brent's lawyer. Since it was uncontested, the divorce was soon final.

As time went by, Bella forgave herself and Brent and moved on with her life. Her cancer went into remission and she returned to work at the hospital. She continued working with the babies and soon her depression was in the past. This was her life's work and she felt rewarded.

Bella also returned to the university and received her master's degree in Family Counseling. She remained Director of Nursing and worked in the nursery every chance she could, but was also able to counsel with the parents of premature or handicapped children. This was a vastly fulfilling occupation.

Brent and Jennifer had married, and they were residing in Chattanooga, Tennessee. He took employment at Erlanger Hospital. The last she heard, Brent was very happy with his new family.

Dear Lord, bless Brent and his family. May they have more children to fill his life with love, Bella prayed. She didn't know if she would ever love or marry again.

CHAPTER SEVENTEEN

The years kept racing by. Kathy and Robert now had three children: two sons and one daughter. They had given them the names Robert Jr., Brandon and Sara. The Hardcastle family had moved to an impressive farmhouse outside of Maryville not far from Kathy's parents. Their marriage was one of gratifying happiness and Bella felt that they were most assuredly blessed.

As Bella was rambling through the closets in her apartment one day, she came across some old photos of her, Kathy, and Thomas that had been taken at a party they all attended in their teen years. Her thoughts returned to that function and how much they had enjoyed it. After thumbing through the snapshots, she felt impressed to phone Kathy and ask her if she had heard anything else about Thomas.

"Hello."

"Kathy, this is Bella. How are you and your family?"

"Oh, Bella, it's so good to hear your voice. We're all fine. How are you?"

"Oh, I'm good, just working hard. Don't have much time for anything else. Sorry I haven't called sooner. The reason I'm calling now is that I was wondering if you have heard any-thing about Thomas lately. He's been in my thoughts a lot and I worry about him."

"Oh, Bella, I'm sorry, too, that I haven't let you know. Last week it was reported to his parents that he is missing in action. A sniper shot down his helicopter over Saigon. I haven't heard anymore. I'm so sorry, Bella, to have to tell you this."

Tears flooded Bella's eyes and she was unable to compose herself.

"Oh, no! Something inside tells me he's still alive!" she said, a tone of assuredness taking over her demeanor. "I refuse to believe he's dead! He's so special to all of us and I've come to realize how much I really care for him. He was the first boy I ever loved."

"Oh, I knew you loved him, Bella. I really think he felt the same way about you. He's written to me several times since he has been in Vietnam and asked about you every time. Let's just pray that he's okay and will come back to us soon." Kathy couldn't help but shed some tears herself.

"If you hear anything, you make sure you let me know, okay?" Bella insisted.

"I will, Bella." Kathy hoped her words of assurance would be at least a minor consolation.

Bella laid the phone down and fell across her bed sobbing heavily.

"*Oh, Lord,*" she prayed with all her heart, "*please bring Thomas back to us soon.*"

Her love for Thomas had returned within her that night and stimulated her emotions to such an extent that she decided she had to do whatever was in her power to try to find him.

The following day she made numerous phone calls to the Red Cross in various areas and one to the Defense Department. They assured her that they were doing all they could to locate the MIAs in Vietnam and nothing else could be done by anyone.

Bella's heart sank as she realized that she may never see Thomas again.

Please, Lord, protect him and give him strength to endure whatever he is going through. Heal him if he is hurt. Amen.

CHAPTER EIGHTEEN

While still on Easter Island, it took Bella a few days to gather the rest of the needed information on the earthquake in Chile, so she utilized the balance of her available time to unwind and do more sightseeing.

But while relaxing, her mind would always wander back into the past. She was now reflecting on the segment of her life after her divorce. By this time Bella was already in her thirties.

The years had been kind to her in appearance because she still appeared surprisingly young. Her eye-catching red hair now was a stylish short cut which was much easier to manage with her busy lifestyle. Her skin was still smooth and lightly-freckled but gave her maturity instead of a childish look. Her slender body shape made her incredibly attractive to men. But she wasn't interested in any man but Thomas. She still had to believe that he was coming home soon. Everyone who really knew her found her very wise and intelligent. On the inside, she had a very spiritual soul filled with love, kindness, compassion, and honesty. She was loved by many. Still, there was an emptiness that needed to be filled; a faith that had waned.

It was now the end of November, 1983, and Bella was looking forward to Christmas vacation this year. Kathy had phoned a week prior and invited her to spend the holidays with her family. She was to drive to their house on Christmas Eve and stay through New Year's Day. There was nobody else with which Bella had rather spend this special season.

Kathy told Bella that she had also invited her parents and her brothers, Josh and Justin, and their families to come for Christmas. Also, Thomas' parents had been invited. Bella had magnificent memories of how much fun she had always had with the McCormick family.

With this in mind, Christmas Day came quickly.

As Bella left home and drove to Kathy's on Christmas Eve, a frosty breeze whistled around her car, puffing in light snow flurries. But there was no real threat on the roads, and the weather even seemed relaxing as she soaked up the enchantment of the lovely Christmas music on the radio. Memories of the past times she had spent with Kathy captivated her thoughts and warmed her soul.

As Bella arrived, she was met with open arms, hugs, and kisses from the families. She carried bundles of gifts as she entered the doorway. Bella was now with friends who always made her feel welcome in their home. They were all very dear to her heart.

Bella noticed that the house was adorned with beautiful, homespun Christmas decorations of poinsettias, holly branches, and mistletoe. The Christmas tree held ornaments the children had made themselves of popcorn garland, candy canes, gingerbread men, and ribbons. So many gifts covered the space underneath the tree that one could not even see the floor. Aromas of turkey, ham, sweet potatoes, sage cornbread dressing, apple and pecan pies, and many other delicious dishes being prepared filled the air.

Now this is what a home is all about, Bella thought.

While the fireplace roared with sparkling flames that matched the warmth Bella had in her heart for these people, there was a rapid knock at the door.

"My, my," said Kathy with a smile, "I wonder who that could be."

"Bella," Robert said, "would you please see who that is?"

Bella quickly rose from her seat and followed his bidding. As she opened the door, she stepped back, gasping in surprise.

"Oh, Thomas!" Bella chimed with excitement. "How? When? Where?" Her mind was overflowing with questions. At that moment, Bella noticed a wisp of a girl approximately six years old standing beside Thomas that obviously was from Southeast Asia. She had long, straight jet black hair and big brown eyes that looked up at Bella with an innocent shyness.

With only a smile, Thomas entered the doorway and was welcomed by Kathy's family.

Thomas' parents knew about the surprise, but were still ecstatic to see him.

"Oh, God has blessed us this Christmas by bringing you home," Thomas' mom said. Her heart was leaping with joy. Although she had seen Thomas once since his return, it still seemed like a dream.

"We knew Thomas was back, Bella, but wanted it to be a surprise for you. Isn't it GREAT?!!! exclaimed Kathy.

"Come, Thomas, and sit. We want to hear all that has happened," Robert said, with a little hesitation. He wasn't sure if Thomas would want to talk about the war.

As Thomas started into the family room, the little girl followed. He took her hand and pulled her to his lap.

"Everybody, this is my daughter, LuAnn. Her mother was a girl I met in Thailand. She died giving birth to LuAnn."

Bella gasped. *What a lovely child.*

"While I was in Vietnam," Thomas began, "our helicopter was shot down by a sniper over

Saigon. There were three soldiers in my troop that were killed and the rest of us were taken to the prison camp in Hao Lo, which we all called the Hanoi Hilton. Conditions there were horrifying! Several prisoners were severely beaten over and over and some of them died. The ones of us who didn't die were left to treat our own wounds, and many got infected because of the filth in the quarters in which we had to live. We had no choice but to lay in our own vomit and feces. Food was scarce, so we very seldom were fed. Some died from starvation. There were only two of us left when the release came.

"In 1973," Thomas continued, "we were released during 'Operation Homecoming.' They transported me to a hospital in Thailand where I spent six months recuperating from my malnutrition and wounds. Not only was my physical health affected, but also my mental health. I decided I would stay in Thailand until I was well enough to come home.

"While in the hospital, I met LuAnn's mother, Mai. We had a relationship and LuAnn was born. Like I said before, she died in childbirth.

Knowing she wouldn't be around, Mai made me promise to take care of LuAnn and always keep her with me. I have kept that promise."

There wasn't a dry eye in the house. These people had hearts of gold filled with much compassion and understanding. They knew why Thomas did what he did.

"One reason I decided to come back to the States is because I want LuAnn to know my friends and family."

At that time, LuAnn left the adult conversation and went to play with the children.

"Another reason for my return is," Thomas said in a softer tone, with sadness in his voice, "LuAnn is sick with leukemia and I have to get her some medical help. I know that East Tennessee Children's Hospital in Knoxville is one of the best in the country. She has an appointment already next week with a Specialist. Please help me pray that they will cure her of this terrible disease. She is my life and I would just die if I lost her," he said as he put his head in his hands and sobbed.

Bella's entire being cried out to Thomas. She knew how it felt to lose a child. LuAnn was such a sweet little girl and Bella had to find the faith within herself to pray, believing God would heal her.

As the guests departed at the end of the evening, Thomas asked Bella if he could stay and talk to her for a while. LuAnn was asleep on the couch by now.

"I can take LuAnn up to the guest room, Thomas," Robert offered, "and you two can sit down here and get to know each other again. Thomas, you can sleep in the room with LuAnn. Bella, your room is down the hallway from there."

Thomas agreed. Robert said goodnight and turned and walked away, cradling LuAnn in his arms.

Bella smiled with joy to have this opportunity to converse with Thomas.

"Now," said Thomas inquisitively, "how has your life been, Bella?"

Bella looked at Thomas and as their eyes met, she began to weep.

"Oh, Thomas, things haven't been the way I dreamed they would be. I married a wonderful man with whom I thought I was going to spend the rest of my life. We had plans to start a family in a few years but it didn't happen. We wanted children very much. "

Thomas' eyes silently spoke volumes.

"Then," Bella continued, "I got uterine cancer, went through a lot of depression and took too many pain pills. Brent just couldn't handle the crisis and neither could I. He had an affair with a nurse and had a baby. We still had feelings for each other but he needed to have children. His heart was empty without them. You understand since you have LuAnn. So he asked me for a divorce and we went our separate ways."

"Did you ever tell Brent that your son's birth was a result of rape?" asked Thomas.

"No, I just never could find the right time," Bella said gruelingly. "Now I wish I had, but I don't think that would have made a difference. He would have done the same thing."

"Thomas, I feel that I have to be honest with you. I've always had deep feelings for you and I didn't realize it until I heard about you being 'missing in action'. A part of me was out there with you and I just knew you would come back to me. I prayed for your safe return every night. After giving it some thought, I know now I really am in love with you and probably have been since the first time we met."

Thomas looked at her with adoration in his eyes.

"Bella, I have always loved you, too. I wrote Kathy many times while I was in Vietnam and told her how I felt about you. She told me you got married and were happy, so I didn't want to interfere. But now, may I tell you what I have wanted so long to say?"

"Of course," Bella said happily. Her heart was racing and was full of devotion to him.

"Bella," Thomas said, "I love you with all my heart. Could we start dating again and really get to know each other? I want LuAnn to get to know you as well."

"She's such a wonderful, beautiful little girl," Bella remarked, "and I know we will love each other. It's so tragic about her mother, but I'm so happy you're both here now."

They reached out and embraced each other with all the love within their souls, kissing sincerely — for the first time.

CHAPTER NINETEEN

Several days remained in the Christmas vacation for Bella, Thomas, Kathy, and Robert. Evangelist James Robison was conducting a crusade at Neyland Stadium in Knoxville the next Friday evening, and they all decided to attend. LuAnn would stay overnight with Josh's family. She became acquainted quickly with his children.

In the days leading up to the crusade, Thomas and Bella spent a lot of time together getting to know one another in a way they had never done before; their likes and dislikes; their emotions; their family backgrounds, etc. Thomas poured out his heart to Bella. He spoke freely about Mai, LuAnn's mother, and her family; Thai culture and history; lifestyles of the modern Thai people; and his life in their captivating land. The two of them took extensive drives through the scenic East Tennessee countryside, enjoying the marvelous handiwork of our Lord God in the snow-covered trees bowing their heads as if praising their Creator. The rural roads seemed to go on forever and they both cherished the relaxing atmosphere.

The evening of the crusade was cold and wintry, but Bella and her friends felt a powerful magnetic force compelling them to attend. They drove the short distance from Maryville to Knoxville, conversing with each other and enjoying the last moments they may have before the end of their vacation.

When the quartet arrived at the crusade, the crowd was enormous. Parking was almost impossible, but they were able to find a space a few blocks away. The frigid temperature was very invigorating to their spirit; and by the time of their arrival, they were ready to listen and take every minute of the crusade into their hearts.

The stadium was overcrowded and extra seating had to be put in place. Smiles crossed everyone's face and it was obvious they were excited to be there.

Evangelist James Robison came onto the stage and everyone stood and applauded. His reputation preceded him. He was truly a man of God and still is today.

As Bella and her friends sat in awe of the power of the message, "Finding Your Purpose in Life," Bella could feel a tug at her heart. She realized that for the past few years, her faith had not been as strong as she wanted it to be. Thomas reached over and took Bella's hand. When their eyes met, he knew instinctively what she was feeling.

The Bible became real to Bella for the first time. Grandma had taught her the Golden Rule, the Ten Commandments, and other scriptures that would remain etched in her heart forever; but this night, it became clear to her what she wanted to do.

As Evangelist Robison offered the invitation to anybody who wanted to make a commitment to the Lord, Bella and Thomas rose from their seats and made the long walk down to the front of the stage. They surrendered their lives to Christ and made a rededication to do the Lord's work. It was clear to them now that their "purpose" was to do God's will. Other people were coming by hundreds from every direction to make a commitment to God. Some were coming for healing of the body.

Bella and Thomas knelt at the front of the stage along with Evangelist Robison and asked God to fill them with His Spirit and give them the strength to do His will. As they prayed, Bella felt God speak to her heart and say He wanted her to become His servant. Knowing she would have to make some changes in her life, she was willing to follow Him in obedience.

On the drive home, Bella and Thomas discussed the dedication to God they had both made. Thomas told Bella he felt the Lord had spoken to him and wanted him to become a missionary.

What would be better than serving the Lord, Bella thought later when she was alone at home.

CHAPTER TWENTY

After the Christmas holiday was over, Bella set out for home and returned to work. She excitedly presented to her co-workers the news of Thomas' heroic return from Vietnam. They expressed their pleasure and gratitude for his safe homecoming.

Bella also shared the commitment she and Thomas made at Evangelist James Robison's crusade for Christ. Needless to say, everybody was thrilled for them and would pray for the right decisions to be made. Bella and Thomas both knew they could not carry out this commitment until LuAnn's cancer was in remission.

Thomas was on cloud nine as he went about his work that next week. He had been granted employment within days after his return at the K-25 Plant in Oak Ridge as a Security Guard on second shift. The commute was some distance from home, but he wanted to remain in

Maryville to provide LuAnn the chance to stay with his parents and form a bond with them.

As the days went by, Bella and Thomas stayed in touch with each other and dated every weekend. Thomas had the responsibility of taking LuAnn for her chemotherapy during the week at East Tennessee Children's Hospital in Knoxville, then working at his job at Oak Ridge in the evenings.

LuAnn's treatments were going very well, although she experienced some nausea immediately after undergoing each chemo. It was unsure how many treatments would be needed, but everyone was praying for her to go through it quickly.

Several months elapsed and the relationship between Bella and Thomas grew with more affection every day. LuAnn came to care for Bella almost as much as Thomas had. The love was mutual that Bella had for LuAnn, and their bond was undeniable.

It was a peaceful Saturday evening the following April. It had been one of those enthralling spring days in which the fluffy clouds float gaily overhead and the song of the robins awaken the romance within the hearts of shy young lovers.

Bella and Thomas were on a date at her apartment. Dinner of pot roast with carrots and potatoes was ending, and Bella was dishing out the cherry cheesecake. Nervously, Thomas pulled a tiny box from his pants pocket, smiled, and leaned across the table toward her.

"Bella, will you marry me?" he whispered, as he flipped up the lid.

"What is this?" Bella gasped in disbelief.

Before Thomas could answer, Bella jumped from her seat, tossed her arms around Thomas' neck and plastered him with an intense kiss that he wished would never end.

"Yes, yes, of course I will marry you!" Bella said breathlessly. "This is what I have dreamed about for a long time. God has blessed us with each other and we are truly soul mates, I believe that."

Thomas reached over the table and put the ring on Bella's hand.

"Then let's tell everyone and set a date as soon as possible," Thomas said eagerly. "I want you as my wife—soon."

"What will LuAnn say?" Bella questioned. "She is a part of this, too, you know!"

"Yes, I agree. She is," Thomas said, "but she loves you almost as much as I do and she'll be thrilled. One thing, though. She will, for sure, want to be the flower girl," he said as his lips formed a smug smile.

"That can be arranged," Bella said, returning the smile. There was only a brief pause before she began again.

"Oh, Thomas," Bella was ecstatic, "you have made me the happiest woman in the world! I couldn't ask for a better man to be my husband."

As soon as Bella arrived back home, she phoned Kathy and Robert to tell them the latest news. They were overjoyed, but told her they had been expecting this to happen.

Bella flashed the engagement ring to her co-workers when she returned to work the following Monday. As they glared in awe, the question came up as to the date of the wedding.

"We haven't set a date yet," Bella said reluctantly, "but it will be soon."

Bella and Thomas couldn't tolerate being apart the next week. They spoke on the phone two and three times every day. The excitement was overwhelming, but they knew they would be together permanently very soon.

CHAPTER TWENTY-ONE

The next Saturday, Thomas drove to Bella's apartment, picked her up, went to the court-house, and they were married that day.

The wedding night was spent in Bella's apartment but it couldn't have been any more romantic if it had been in a honeymoon suite at the Hilton. The passion between them filled the room and their bed.

Thomas is truly the love of my life that the Good Lord has sent to me. What a blessing! I will do whatever I have to do to be everything he needs. Thank you, Jesus, Bella said to herself the next morning as she lay in bed.

That afternoon, Bella and Thomas drove to Maryville to gather Thomas' possessions and pick up LuAnn. The news was quickly assumed by his parents and they couldn't have been happier. Bella phoned Kathy and Robert and told them about the happy event.

"That's great, Bella!" Kathy said. "I'm glad you didn't have the big wedding this time. Thomas has all the expenses taking care of LuAnn's cancer and we knew money was short. You were meant for each other. Take care of yourself and your family and God will bless your marriage."

"Thank you, Kathy," Bella returned. "Tell Robert and the family hello for me and we'll see you as soon as we can."

"Bella, how is LuAnn coming along with her treatments?"

"She's doing very well although she did get a little nauseous in the beginning. It isn't as bad now. She only has a few more treatments, and the doctors feel she will be cured."

Bella was constantly praying softly in her heart.

"That's great. We'll still keep our prayers going up and have faith that the Lord will heal her," Kathy said. Her words were not just lip service. She truly believed for the answer.

"Thanks, again, Kathy," Bella said, as she hung up the phone. "That means a lot to us."

Bella, Thomas, and LuAnn drove back to Bella's apartment with Thomas and LuAnn's belongings. Bella knew it would be cramped quarters for a while until they could find a larger house to purchase, but at least they would be together.

In the weeks following the marriage, it was decided Bella would ask for a job transfer from Baptist Hospital in Knoxville to East Tennessee Children's Hospital to make it more convenient for her to be with LuAnn during her chemo treatments. The transfer was granted and a big party was held on Bella's last day as Director of Nursing and Family Counselor at Baptist. Tears were shed by everyone she had befriended through the years she had been employed there. But she knew she was doing the right thing with the transfer.

East Tennessee Children's Hospital was proud to have Bella as their employee now. Administration soon made her Director of Pediatric Nursing, as the current Director was retiring. She was caring for the babies again. She couldn't be happier. This is where Bella's heart was in her career.

LuAnn underwent five more chemo treatments. The doctors reported the cancer was in remission after the fifth treatment.

"Praise the Lord! Praise the Lord!" Bella, Thomas, and LuAnn broke down in tears and hugged each other for what seemed like hours.

Bella and Thomas had a lot to be thankful to God for now. A decision had to be made as to the commitment they made at the crusade several months before.

CHAPTER
TWENTY-TWO

As Thomas proceeded to research information on becoming a missionary, he became very involved in the local ministry in their church. As he spoke with the officials there, he acquired the names of other missionaries he would later contact for their advice and wisdom of the mission field.

Southern Baptist Theological Seminary held religious education classes at First Baptist Church in Lenoir City, Tennessee, which was only a short drive from Knoxville. Thomas decided to attend these classes and prepare for the mission field.

He later went on several brief mission trips to Latin America to obtain the experience he needed in order to understand the sacrifices missionaries had to make. He knew that he would also need to at least learn Spanish for the areas in which he wished to serve. Whatever the need, he committed himself to it.

Through all this training and preparation, Thomas could feel the spirit of the Lord filling his soul every day and with each experience. Bella fully supported him in his endeavors and was very proud of him. She knew, though, the day would come and he would be ready to do God's will in his life. Therefore, he would be leaving for some foreign mission. She had a faint feeling in her soul when she thought of this happening.

Ten years had passed and LuAnn was a teenager. Her love for her father and Bella grew stronger every day. Bella had become the mother LuAnn had never had and their relationship was very dear to both of them. She felt God had blessed her with the best parents a child could have. They were very understanding and compassionate when she needed them to be. Her teen years were filled with nothing but happiness.

Bella would continue her employment at East Tennessee Children's Hospital and reside in Knoxville. LuAnn would live with Bella until she graduated from high school.

Thomas completed his preparation for the mission field. As he explained to Bella and LuAnn where he was expected to go, their hearts felt weak at the thought of his traveling to countries where there were enemies of Christians. But they were warmed by the dedication he had made to do God's will. Even though he would not be away permanently, he would spend slices of his time at home with them as well.

Mission trips took Thomas to Mexico, Belize, Brazil, and numerous other Spanish and Portuguese-speaking Latin American countries to serve the missions of building churches, disaster relief, rescuing refugees, taking medical supplies and food to the sick and hungry, etc., wherever needed. Through this service, he witnessed for the Lord and won hundreds of people to Christ. This service was very fulfilling and rewarding to Thomas. His heart went out to these people and his love was God's "agape" spilling over from his heart.

When Thomas would come home, he would have exciting stories to tell and photographs of the areas he had been to show Bella, LuAnn, and all their friends. The reasons for being there were always different but the people were much the same. They needed help and Thomas and his mission were there to provide that help. People of most countries were accepting of the missionaries and grew to love them. The gratitude they displayed was heart-felt, and Thomas and his team experienced that love and warmth. It was a blessing from God.

Bella would sit and listen to the stories with both *fear* and *joy* in her heart. She knew Thomas was providing a service to the people and was doing God's will, but she still trembled every time he told of the danger they were always in while in these foreign lands.

CHAPTER TWENTY-THREE

While Thomas was home spending some time with his family before leaving on the next mission, he approached Bella when she was alone, cooking in the kitchen one evening. The house was quiet and serene with LuAnn and her friends absent. They were attending a concert in town and she would be late coming home.

"Bella, I have something I need to talk to you about," Thomas began. "It has to do with my next mission."

"What is it, Thomas?" Bella asked quickly. His tone was somber, so she reached out and pulled a chair from the dining table and sat down.

Thomas sat beside her, leaned toward her and grasped her hand.

"You know why I'm on the mission field and why I'm doing what I do, don't you?" Thomas asked with earnestness.

"Of course I do," Bella said. Wonder reflected in her eyes. "Why are you asking me that?"

"Well, I just want you to understand why it's very important to do this, even though I have to leave you and LuAnn at home to take care of yourselves. My family is my life and if I lost you both, I would die! But these people I minister to are also God's people and they need my help along with the rest of the missionaries. They couldn't survive at all without our help. Do you still understand?" Thomas was looking into her soul.

"What are you trying to tell me, Thomas," Bella said fearfully. "Just spit it out!"

"Bella, darling, my next mission is to Colombia, South America, and we will be delivering medical supplies and food to a tribal village there. We'll have to go into areas where the revolutionists are hiding in the jungle. We have to have the faith that God will protect us or we will be martyrs for his kingdom. I hope you *really do* understand and will ask the Lord to bless this mission."

"Oh, Thomas, I'd beg you not to go, but I know you would go anyway." Bella had moisture swelling up in her eyes. "You know how much I support what you do and my heart will go with you. I love you very much and you have been the best thing that has ever happened to me. I really knew this day would come, but I'm still not prepared for it. Just know you will be in my thoughts and prayers every minute of every day."

"Thank you so much." Thomas was overjoyed. "Bella, you know part of my heart is always with you and LuAnn here at home and I pray for you both every day while I am away. My love is always with you also and I really feel blessed to have the opportunity to witness to these people. They have not heard the gospel and the mission wants me to be their translator.

The weeks until Thomas' departure went by quickly. It was now the day—June 12, 1995— and he was ready to leave for the airport. He met the other missionaries there and they boarded the airplane following many hugs, kisses, and tears shed by their families.

"Please be careful and come home to us soon. God bless you all," were the last words these men would hear from their families' voices.

As Thomas and his missionary friends sat on the airplane during take off, they could see their wives and children standing in the windows of the airport waving goodbye. Little did they know, it was their *last goodbye.*

CHAPTER TWENTY-FOUR

Two weeks went by and neither Bella nor the other families heard a word from Thomas and his group. They were, needless to say, getting antsy and worried. The authorities were contacted but could not gather any information about the whereabouts or the safety of the mission. The village they were attempting to reach was in such a remote area there was no communication anywhere nearby. Transportation was scarce, so they had to walk much of the way. The jungles were incredibly dense with trees and plants; it was difficult to even walk. Many stops would have to be made in order to eat, sleep, and rest. The trip could take up to three weeks to just reach the village.

The authorities suggested the family be patient and wait at least another week before being concerned. They assured them they would check into their whereabouts at that time if nothing had been reported.

Bella's heart skipped a beat as she was told what to do, but she felt she had no choice. She had no way of knowing anything until the authorities were contacted.

The next Sunday at their church, she asked the pastor to pray for Thomas and his friends' safety in this perilous situation. The congergation stood up, joined hands, and prayed together the Lord's Prayer, and then the Pastor concluded the petition. Tears filled the eyes of the families involved and Bella felt the faith to accept the fact that the Lord's will would be done, whatever that was for Thomas.

Another week passed without any reports either to the authorities or to the families. Bella felt in her heart the news would not be good when it did come. The authorities reassured Bella they would see what they could find out.

Still another week went by. Then a knock came at the door one Wednesday afternoon when Bella was alone in the house. LuAnn had now graduated from high school and had left for college.

"Mrs. Thomas James?" said a tall man dressed in a dark suit and tie as Bella opened the door.

"Yes, I'm Mrs. James. May I help you?" Bella returned, with a quiver in her voice.

"I have some news about your husband, Thomas. May I come in?" he asked.

"Yes, please," Bella said as she stepped back and opened the door wider.

"Please, sir, what have you heard?" Bella began. "Is Thomas alright?"

"I'm sorry, Mrs. James, Thomas' body has been found by some journalists working in the Colombia area about five miles from the village where they were taking the food and medical supplies. The bodies of the other missionaries and a guide they had hired to take them there were found also." As he continued, the expression on his face was one of remorse and deep sadness.

"It was told to us by the journalists that the missionaries had been captured by revolutionaries and taken to their camp. There it appeared they were beaten and shot in the back to make it look as if they were trying to escape. The revolutionaries stole all the food and medical supplies from them for their own use, so the village was never provided for. The authorities feel guilty for sending Thomas and his friends into that remote area knowing the guerillas were there and that this might happen. That was a chance we all chose to take in order to get the village the help they needed. The missionaries knew the danger but they wanted to help the people so they volunteered to take that risk. They were ALL very brave men. Just remember that. Your husband was a remarkable man of God."

Bella was quiet—as if an arrow had pierced her and stopped her in her steps.

The man continued, "Please realize how much he will be blessed in God's kingdom to die as a martyr and how much we were all blessed to have him."

"Yes, I know that, we were all blessed and he was a very brave man," Bella said trying to hold back the tears. Her heart was melting. Her soul mate and love of her life was gone. She had wished she had tried harder to stop him from going to Colombia, but she knew in her heart she couldn't have done that. He was determined to go. He had a purpose and it was God's purpose and he gave his life trying to carry it out.

"Again, Mrs. James, I am so sorry. You have the sympathy of the entire organization. I have to leave now and visit the other missionaries' families. We will call you with the details of when their bodies will arrive at the airport. It will take a few days to get everything processed through to the U.S. but it won't be long, I assure you." He reached out and took her hand and looked in her face with earnest conviction. "God bless you and your family, Mrs. James."

Bella, still in shock, slowly closed the door behind her and fell onto the couch, sobbing her heart out.

God, why did you let this happen? He was serving you and you let him down! I don't understand. I thought I did but I don't! All I know is he is gone, my darling husband is gone forever. How will I tell LuAnn? She will be devastated.

That night, Bella was comforted by members of the church as they began to call her on the phone and give their condolences. They gave her the strength and encouragement she needed to get through this crisis. She began to feel a weight lifting off her heart and she felt she could control herself enough to phone LuAnn. She dialed the number to LuAnn's dorm.

"Hello," Bella said, as a young lady answered the phone. "Could I please speak to LuAnn James? This is her mother and it's an emergency."

"Yes, just a moment and I'll get her," said the young lady.

"Yes, Mother," LuAnn said quickly, "what's wrong?"

"I have some bad news about your father," Bella said sadly. "I got a visit today from a man that works with the authorities in Colombia, South America. He said some journalists working in the jungles there found the bodies of your father and the other missionaries five miles from the village where they were delivering medical supplies and food. They had been captured by revolutionaries and taken to a camp. They had been beaten and then shot in the back. Oh, LuAnn, he's gone! I can't believe he's gone!" Bella's voice trailed as she began to weep uncontrollably.

"Oh, no, Mother!" LuAnn couldn't accept it. "He can't be! How are we going to live without him?" LuAnn was also crying hysterically.

"You know he was doing God's will and just trying to help those people in the village," Bella was doing all she could to encourage and comfort LuAnn, but was it enough? "He was a very brave man and we have to remember that about him. He didn't just love us but he loved all God's people. He was a remarkable man of God. Just remember, too, that he loved you with all his heart. He will be returned to us as soon as all the details are covered and the authorities can bring him back. LuAnn, please come home. We need each other right now."

"Of course, I will be there in the morning. Get a good night's sleep and don't worry. We will take care of all the arrangements together," LuAnn reassured Bella.

Bella fell into bed with a heavy heart, knowing what was ahead for her and the other families of the missionaries.

Please, Lord, help us all get through this crisis. Help the children know that their fathers died serving you and trying to help others. Amen.

CHAPTER TWENTY-FIVE

Bella awoke the next morning to a sunny day outside but a very murky darkness in her life. As she lay in bed awake, she began to imagine the torment Thomas and the other missionaries had gone through the last days of their lives. It must have been horrifying!! She knew the bodies would be too mutilated to open the coffins.

At that moment, the phone rang. Bella jumped out of bed and ran to answer it.

"Hello," she said breathlessly.

"Hello, Mrs. James," said the voice of a man on the other end of the line.

"Yes, this is she," said Bella. The voice sounded like the man that visited her from the authorities.

"The remains of Thomas James and the other missionaries will be delivered to their individual funeral homes by the end of next week," the man said in a professional tone. "What funeral home will you be using?"

"Haven of Rest Funeral Home in Maryville, Tennessee. Thomas' family lives there and that is where he would want to go. I will contact them and let them know he is coming. They know about his death already."

She had asked Thomas' parents to call Kathy and Robert and relay the news. She just hadn't felt up to talking to them that first day.

As Bella went through her chores the next day, she felt numb all over. The phone rang and stunned her from her thoughts.

"Hello," she answered.

"Hello, Bella," responded Kathy. "Oh, honey, I am so sorry to hear about Thomas. Are you doing okay?"

Bella could hardly respond. Kathy could tell she was weeping faintly, but she heard a muffled, tiny voice saying, "Not really."

"I'll be there tomorrow to help you with the arrangements. This is a time you need friends and family with you. Is LuAnn coming home soon?"

"Uh-huh." Bella was really glad Kathy called, though she was not at herself. "She'll be here today. We're both in shock. Even though we knew this could happen, it just doesn't seem real. Thomas was so dear to both of us and now he is gone." She began to cry harder. "I am so glad you're coming, Kathy. You will be a big help."

"You know I love you and you are a dear friend to me. I will be there no matter what." Kathy comforted Bella with these words. "Thomas was a very good man of God, a loving husband and father. He died doing God's work and serving other people that couldn't help themselves. He had a lot of courage and strength."

LuAnn came home later that day. Bella met her at the door with embraces and tears. As they sat and talked about all the good times they had with Thomas, the burden lifted from their hearts to some degree. No bad memories of Thomas; only good ones.

Kathy arrived the next day carrying a heavy burden for Bella and LuAnn which was as evident as if it had been a visible weight on her shoulders. Robert was unable to come because of work and taking care of the farm. Their children were also grown and out of the house, either going to college or working a job.

The ladies spent the day relaxing and enjoying each other's company. The comfort they received from one another was heartening. The future seemed a little brighter the following day.

Bella phoned the funeral home and made an appointment with the funeral director to discuss the arrangements of Thomas' funeral service.

As the appointment approached, Bella asked LuAnn and Kathy to go with her. Of course they said they would.

"Please sit down everyone," said Mr. Davis, Funeral Director at Haven of Rest Funeral Home.

"I received a phone call from the authorities yesterday that they are bringing Thomas' remains back to Maryville. They said he would arrive Thursday afternoon around 3:00. You will need to come by here and identify him and collect any personal belongings of his which they may have. Will you be able to do that?" he asked.

"Of course we will," Bella said as she handed Mr. Davis a list of Thomas' wishes he had given her before he started on his mission trips. He knew that he may not come back some day and didn't want the arrangements to be a burden on Bella and LuAnn.

"One request he mentioned was a closed coffin. Make sure ALL his wishes are carried out, okay?" Bella asked.

"Sure, we will," answered Mr. Davis.

Bella, LuAnn, and Kathy left the funeral home in silence. The experience was humbling. They returned to Bella's apartment, prepared dinner, ate, and went to bed. The evening went quickly, but all three women slept like babies that night. The rest was much needed and welcomed.

All family and friends were notified as to when the funeral was to be held. Thursday afternoon was soon there and it was time for the service.

All guests were greeted by Bella and LuAnn. Each gave hugs and condolences. Thomas had many friends. The eulogy was given by the pastor at the church that supported Thomas' mission trips and where he and Bella were members for many years. The service was superbly done. He told of Thomas' bravery in dying as a martyr doing the Lord's will. The details of his death were given and Bella could hear all the gasps from the people who didn't know. "The agape love Thomas had for his family and for God's family was remarkable. He was always there with a helping hand, whether it be physical or emotional. He has gone to his reward. One day we will meet him again."

Pastor explained the time Thomas spent in the P.O.W. camp while in the Vietnam War and the horrible torment he had endured there.

"He lived through many troubles and trials in his life, but the Lord had a purpose for him to serve His will. That is why he came home after Vietnam," the pastor stated with sincerity.

At the end of the service, the family rode in the special car provided by the mortuary to the graveyard where Thomas was being laid to rest. The exquisite flowers were gathered and laid around the coffin. Thomas would have been happy to see his family and friends all there. Even people from Knoxville that didn't know him personally but felt a connection to him through the publicity the mission trips had received in the local newspaper had come.

After the graveside service was over, the funeral director came over to Bella. He handed her what appeared to be a letter.

"This was found in Thomas' shirt pocket after he was delivered to us. It was among his personal effects but for some reason was not given to you earlier," he told her softly, so no one else could hear.

Bella took the envelope and quickly opened it. She could see it *was* a letter to her and LuAnn from Thomas. As Bella silently read, her heart was torn apart.

My dearest Bella,

If you are reading this letter, it means I am dead. I am sorry, My Darling, Bella. I know you are hurting deeply right now because of my decision to do this. Please forgive me, but I know you understand why I did it.

Before we were captured, we did have the opportunity to witness to several villagers in Colombia. After arriving at the airport, we were sent to deliver food to a village nearby that the guerillas did not occupy. They welcomed us with open arms. There were approximately 75 to 100 villagers. The hunger was horrific! Many had died already from starvation. It touched my heart and brought tears to my eyes to receive many hugs and thanks of gratitude from them. We stayed a few days and were able to read the Bible to them and tell them about Jesus. Many were converted to Christ during this time.

So, Bella, don't think this mission was in vain. Although we weren't able to reach the village we were sent to, God provided a way for us to witness to these people. Praise God for what He did.

While we are being held captive in the guerilla camp, my heart has been full of regrets that I would likely never see you again. You are my true love, my soul mate, and I praise God every day for bringing us together. Your love has been what always gave me the strength to make these mission trips. Each time, I counted the days till we would be together again. I am afraid that won't happen this time. I know my time is near. We heard the soldiers talking last night and we know they are going to kill us. We are ready to go and meet our Lord.

Please, Bella, don't fret too much. You need your strength to continue on in your life and continue God's will. LuAnn will need you to be strong and comfort her. Just keep the faith and hope you get from the Lord God Almighty.

My love forever,

Thomas

P.S. There is also a letter to LuAnn enclosed. Please see that she gets it for me.

Bella's eyes overflowed with tears as she handed the other letter to LuAnn.

My dearest daughter, LuAnn,

Your hurting is unbearable for you right now, I know, but don't think I died in vain. Many came to know the Lord as their Savior on this mission and I do not have any regrets that I came.

Your mother will tell you what happened on the trip. It is in her letter. But don't have any hard feelings toward the ones who killed us. We have to learn to forgive our enemies.

We will be in a better place soon. We have heard the guerillas talking and we know we will soon go to be with the Lord. We are ready to meet Him and know that we gave our lives for His will.

Please know I will always love you and will watch over you. You have been with me all your life and I will never leave you. You are my Special Little Girl.

Please take care of Bella for me and see that she is happy in the days to come. Find a good man and have children. Remember your education and use it for God's purpose.

Don't fret; keep smiling.

Love, Dad

They clutched the letters to their hearts and wept together. As they reached out and held each other, they felt Thomas' love flowing through them. What an amazing man! He had so much love to bestow upon everyone.

Bella prayed that night, *Well, Lord, it is the end of another era of my life now. Please help me find the next one. Help me also to discover my "mission" to carry on through Thomas vicariously.*

CHAPTER TWENTY-SIX

After graduating with honors from the University of Tennessee in Knoxville, LuAnn continued her education by attending UT's Graduate School of Medicine for her preparation in becoming an M.D. While in medical school, she met a student, Jeffery Winters, whom she dated for two years, then married. They were able to continue their studies and graduate together.

LuAnn decided she wanted to specialize in Pediatrics and Jeffery, Internal Medicine in Geriatrics.

The couple started practicing in a walk in clinic caring for people of low-income and the elderly. Many patients were suffering from malnutrition. It was very rewarding to witness these patients begin to grow stronger every day from their treatments, and in time, were able to live productive lives.

The children would begin to develop normally and their learning abilities would improve enormously.

179

LuAnn and Jeffery would take every opportunity to invite their patients to church with them. Many came to know Jesus as their Savior and changed their lives.

As time went on, LuAnn and her husband, Jeffery, grew in their spiritual walk with God. They also used their professions to serve God in every aspect of their lives. Thomas would have been proud.

Bella returned to work in a short time. Emotionally, she was still grieving, but somehow managed to function at her job. Caring for the babies always put a smile on her face and joy in her heart. She spent as many hours at the hospital as she could, putting in considerable overtime.

As she was diligently working in her office, lost in paperwork one day, the Administrator of the hospital, Mr. Waters, rapped briskly on her door.

"Come in," said Bella, as her eyes darted to the source of the knock.

"Hi, Bella," Mr. Waters smiled as he came in and sat down. "Could I speak with you for just a few minutes?"

"Of course," Bella replied, with wonder in her tone.

"The Board of Directors of the hospital, the staff, and the employees have met and discussed a project I would like to bring to your attention."

Bella could sense something good was about to happen. She just seemed to have a gift for perception. She allowed a tiny smile to form on her lips before he finished.

"We want to dedicate a room in the hospital to Thomas. He was such a great Christian man with such strong convictions. We all loved him and respected him very much. It was a devastating loss when he was taken from us. But we know he was doing the Lord's will. Therefore, we thought the Chapel would be a good room. We would hang a plaque on the door with his name, profession, and dates of his birth and death. Would you approve?" Mr. Waters looked at Bella with a serious look in his eyes waiting for her answer.

By now Bella had tears streaming down her face.

"Of course I approve," she said excitedly. "I would be honored and it touches my heart deeply to know my friends and co-workers thought that much of Thomas. Everybody that knew him loved him and he loved everybody. He truly *was* a remarkable man."

"I'm so sorry for your loss," said Mr. Waters. "Do you know what's ahead for you in life?"

"I plan on living one day at a time. But there is something I have always dreamed of doing when I get the opportunity," Bella said smiling through the tears.

"What is that?" asked Mr. Waters.

"I have always been interested in and have done some studies in astronomy. Some day it is my dream to experience a total eclipse of the sun. It may be necessary to travel some distance to see it, but I will do that no matter what the circumstances," Bella said with confidence.

"Wow, that would be great!" exclaimed Mr. Waters.

"You deserve to live all your dreams," Mr. Waters said. As he walked to the door, he turned and smiled at Bella. "Take care of yourself and if I can help you in any way, please let me know."

"I certainly will on both accounts. Thanks," said Bella with gratitude in her voice.

CHAPTER TWENTY-SEVEN

The alarm loudly sounded on Bella's clock at 4:00 a.m. that morning on Easter Island, waking her from a deep sleep. She jumped from her bed knowing she had to catch her flight to Santiago, Chile in just over two hours. Her suitcases were packed the night before and the clothes she had chosen to wear were lying on her wooden chest at the bottom of her bed.

Previously, she had called the Red Cross authorities in Chile about the need for nurses there. Her Spanish was mediocre, so she had been thrilled to find that the director, Mr. Ian Richards, spoke English. She described her qualifications to him and he was very impressed. After all, she had been in the nursing profession for over thirty years. Her love for people and God was overwhelming and the Red Cross director could hear it in her voice.

"One organization we work closely with is Doctors Without Borders, Mr. Richards told her, "and you will be working with them as much as possible."

"That would be great," Bella replied with excitement "They are a fantastic organization, and I would be thrilled and honored to be a part of their staff."

"I really feel in my heart and soul this is where God wants me to be at this time in my life. I have done a lot of praying about this. It has always been a dream of mine to see an eclipse of the sun so that is why I came to Easter Island. One day, I decided to take a trip to Santiago to witness the devastation for myself. It was overwhelming and horrific! As soon as I returned to Easter Island, it was my desire to find out from your office what I could do to help. I've been a Red Cross volunteer in the U.S. for some time now."

Mr. Richards told Bella any help she could give would be appreciated. Nurses and doctors were both needed in all fields. There were hundreds of people that still needed attention.

Therefore, Bella decided to leave on the first flight the very next day. Excitement was flowing through her body so intensely she had a glow on her face.

She boarded the airplane and took her seat. The flight would take approximately four and a half hours to reach Santiago. The pilot announced that the weather was extremely sunny and pleasant for the day and the flight should be very smooth.

Bella's seat was next to the window, so she basked in the relaxed atmosphere, peering through the round pane at the transparent fluffy clouds and pristine blue sky.

Her mind began to again drift back to the past. She was reminiscing about a time several years after Thomas' death.

It was now August, 2001. Bella was semi-retired from the nursing profession at East Tennessee Children's Hospital. She had made the decision to do some traveling to places she had always dreamed of seeing.

Bella was touring New York City, the Big Apple, with a group of friends from her church. Visiting heralded sights, such as the Empire State Building, the Statue of Liberty, Museum of Modern Art, Central Park, and the American Museum of Natural History were a given in their plans. A one day excursion to Niagara Falls was also on the agenda. The women looked forward to a day of shopping on Fifth Avenue.

The group enjoyed vacationing together and took the opportunity to get more acquainted with each other.

After Bella and the church group returned home, one month passed until the day America will never forget. It is called, "the 102 minutes that changed America."

On September 11, 2001, 19 al-Qaeda terrorists hijacked four U.S. commercial passenger airliners. The hijackers intentionally crashed two of the airliners into the Twin Towers of the World Trade Center in New York City, killing everyone on board and many others working in the Twin Towers. Both buildings collapsed within two hours, also destroying nearby buildings and damaging others.

Bella, along with all Americans, couldn't believe their eyes when they saw the actual event happen on television. *What is going to happen now? How will the United States recover from this?* Bella wondered as she looked on in shock.

Bella's heart bled for the families of the people who died in this tragedy. Since she was a Red Cross volunteer, she was called to join them in traveling to New York City to help with the medical aid needed.

She had hurt with the natives of Haiti when the terrible quake had rocked their country earlier in 2010, but for some reason had not felt the call to go. The time just wasn't right — now it was different. Perhaps it was because it was in the area of Thomas' missions.

Her heart was desperately going out to the people of Chile now. All three of these horrific tragedies left many people without the loved ones they relied upon for their livelihood and emotional support. Many children lost their parents; parents lost children; husbands lost wives; wives lost husbands; siblings lost siblings. Words cannot describe the permanent wound left in the hearts of these people. The grieving process would be a long one for many.

With feelings of families on her mind, her thoughts turned to LuAnn, Jeffery, and their children; one son, Shaun, and one daughter, Mia. Bella felt very blessed to have this family.

Bella's mind wondered to her father, who had not entered her thoughts in a long time. She still wondered of his whereabouts and his health. He would be getting up in age by now. *Does he ever think of me? Does he wonder where I am and if I am okay?* These were questions she would like to have answered one day.

Dad, I still need you in my life. Please be out there where I can find you? I have faith I will someday.

CHAPTER TWENTY-EIGHT

As the plane touched down in Santiago, Bella felt an urgency to reach someone who could tell her where to go to help the earthquake victims. She located the Red Cross Center downtown, went inside and asked for Mr. Ian Richards. It was only a couple of minutes till Mr. Richards entered the room from an office located to the right of the front door.

"May I help you?" Mr. Richards asked, while motioning for Bella to sit down.

"My name is Bella James and I am the nurse who spoke with you earlier from Easter Island. As you know, I have witnessed the devastation and am looking forward to working with you."

"It's good to meet you! I remember our conversation and have given it much thought as to where you can serve the most at this time," said Mr. Richards, smiling and reaching to shake her hand. "I will have a Red Cross volunteer escort you to one of the field hospitals and introduce you to the staff. Would you follow me, please?"

As Bella walked behind Mr. Richards, she felt tense not knowing what she was facing. He led her to an office down the hallway of the Red Cross Center. When he opened the door of the office, there sat a young man who appeared to be in his twenties, dark hair and dark eyes, slim build, with a pile of paperwork on his desk.

"Hi, Mr. Richards," the young man said. "What can I do for you today?"

"Hello, Randy, this is Bella James. She is a Registered Nurse from the United States and wishes to join up with the "Doctors Without Borders" to assist with the injured and homeless."

"Hi, Ms. James, my name is Randy Evans. I can escort you to the location of the doctors. It isn't a pretty sight, I will warn you."

"Please call me Bella and thanks, I would appreciate the escort. That is why I am here, to help," she replied with a smile.

"OK, let's go," said Randy, as he walked toward the door with Bella following close behind.

"It was nice making your acquaintance, Ms. James," Mr. Richards said quickly, nodding. "I'm sure we will see each other again."

As Bella and Randy drove to the field hospital, the conversation turned to a more personal nature.

"Where did you live in the U.S.," Randy asked, "I am originally from Iowa."

"Tennessee," Bella answered proudly. "I was born in McMinnville; then moved to Maryville when I was six years old. I am a true Southern Belle."

"Well, nothing wrong with that. I hear you're very special ladies. If they all look like you, they must be very pretty ones, too," Randy blushed.

Soon they arrived at the site of the field hospital. As they entered, Bella and Randy could see all the injured and dying lying on cots provided by the Red Cross. Many had IV drip tubes attached to one arm while others were hooked to oxygen tubes. There were patients missing limbs; many with bandages covering their heads; others lying very quietly; several were moaning from severe pain.

It was heart rendering to Bella to see these people suffering. Many of them were children and of course, that is where Bella's heart beats the loudest. She stopped along the way between patients to speak to them and introduce herself. She would speak words of encouragement and try to bring smiles to their faces.

Randy walked Bella to an office that was located toward the rear of the hospital. The man that was seated in the office noticed them and came out to greet them.

"Hi, Randy, what are you doing here?" the gentleman asked as he extended his hand.

"Well," Randy answered, "I brought you some help. This is Bella James from the United States. She's a Registered Nurse and wanted to donate her time to assist the Doctors Without Borders. Of course, I thought of you."

"Bella," Randy continued, "meet Dr. Michael Brooks. He is the Chief of Staff here at the field hospital, a very busy man. But he loves every minute of it, right?"

Dr. Brooks wagged his head in agreement and followed, sporting a tiny grin.

"Bella, you'll be very busy, too. I hope you don't mind hard work."

"Not at all," Bella jumped in. "In fact, I welcome it. I would love to take care of the children, if I may," she said with enthusiasm.

"That would be great!" said Dr. Brooks. "They need so much love and attention, since most of them have been orphaned by this devastation. I feel in my heart you would be really good for them."

Bella had a smile from ear to ear after hearing Dr. Brooks' answer and could hardly wait to start to work.

"Oh, thank you, Dr. Brooks, so much. I won't let you or the children down, I promise."

Bella began treating the children immediately by following Dr. Brooks' instructions. She found the majority of the children were very depressed and grieving from the loss of their family. They had no will to live. The injuries were moderate to severe.

One five-year-old girl, named Arianna, had to have a leg removed from being trapped under a large beam. The rest of her family was all killed by the impact. Arianna soon grew to be very special to Bella.

Bella's heart went out to all these children, especially the ones who were left alone. She wondered what would happen to them after their healing. Where would they go? The local orphanage had sustained damage in the quake. It was already near full capacity, so it could never hold them all, even after repairs were completed.

Bella worked many long, hard hours at the hospital and also did some transfer work in the other field hospitals. She always took care of the children and loved every minute of it although it was somewhat heartbreaking.

Bella not only gave medical help to the children, she gave encouragement, love, hope, and faith. Being the fun-loving person she was, she would enjoy playing games with them when they began to feel better.

Bella was a remarkable person and truly a woman after God's own heart. The strength she found in the Lord got her through every day. Everybody that knew her could see and feel the love she had for those children. Bella had learned some Spanish from Thomas, but she continued her study of the language in her spare time, and was becoming more fluent every day, so she had no problem communicating with all the natives.

Every night when retiring, she would pray to God:

Please, Lord, take care of these children. Heal the ones that need a touch from your hand and the ones that are grieving, please give them comfort, hope, and faith. They are your children, Lord. Lead me to do whatever I can to help them. I ask this prayer in Jesus' name, Amen.

CHAPTER
TWENTY-NINE

It had been several weeks since Bella had contacted LuAnn, so she decided to try to find an operating phone and give her a call. She found one at the Red Cross Center and didn't waste a minute dialing LuAnn's number. With the difference in the time zones, she wasn't sure what hour it would be in Knoxville.

"Hello," LuAnn answered the phone.

"Hello, LuAnn, how are you all doing?" Bella said excitedly.

"Oh, Mom, is that you?" LuAnn could hardly believe her ears.

"Yes, it is! How are you and the family?"

"We're just great! It's so good to hear your voice!" LuAnn remarked with glee. "How is it going with the victims there? Are they getting enough help?"

"Well, it's been slow. Some other countries are pitching in and helping with food and water. The medical supplies are scarce, and we're short of medical staff," Bella said sadly. "The cleanup will take a long time and the construction will be going on for years."

"Oh, I'm so sorry, Mom, I know that is distressing for you. But I know you're doing all you can do. Are you getting to take care of the children?" LuAnn could sense what Bella was feeling because she was a Pediatrician and took care of children in her own practice.

"I've been able to meet many very distinguished doctors and nurses that have volunteered their time to come here and help the victims," Bella said proudly. "Doctors Without Borders is a great organization. They're so sincere in helping these people and really skilled in their specialties."

"That's great and I'm so proud of you for donating your talent and time," LuAnn said from her heart. "You're a remarkable woman, Mom."

This was music to Bella's ears. She was touched by the love she received from LuAnn.

Thomas would be proud of both of them. She wished so much he could be with her. He would have enjoyed helping the victims. Bella knew she wanted to witness to these people just like Thomas would have. They needed to hear about Jesus. She wanted to reach the children with "the Good News." After all, they were the future of their country.

"Well," Bella said, "I better cut this short because of the cost. Tell the family hello for me and I miss you all. Take care and know that I love all of you. Bye."

Bella had tears in her eyes and an empty feeling in her heart.

"Bye, Mom," said LuAnn softly. "We love you, too. Take care of yourself. We miss you."

CHAPTER THIRTY

Bella did miss her family back in the States, but the people of Chile had become her second "familia." The doctors and nurses she worked closely beside had become her friends.

More and more doctors had started coming to assist in the medical aid needed. Bella would get to know them through the Red Cross volunteers, and she made it a point to take the opportunity to introduce herself to them whenever possible.

One day as Bella was taking care of Arianna, one of the nurses, Marianne, approached her. "Bella," Marianne said urgently, "I would like you to meet one of the Red Cross volunteers here in Santiago, Franco Escobar. He's a surgeon and has performed countless operations on the victims of the earthquake. He's a fantastic doctor. A lot of people would have died without his helping hand."

Franco had attended medical college in the United States and therefore, could speak English fluently.

"Pleasure to meet you, Franco," Bella answered with a smile.

Franco was a muscular, well-built, dark-skinned, middle-aged man with thick, graying waves of hair. Bella thought he was very handsome and almost blushed when introduced to him.

"The pleasure is mine," Franco said as he clasped Bella's hand. "I hear you are the 'Florence Nightingale' of the nurses around here."

"Oh, I wouldn't say that," Bella grinned. "I'm just doing what I love to do. The children are my life and I love every one of them with all my heart. When I can help them survive this crisis, whether physically or mentally, I know I've done what the Good Lord sent me here to do. "

"Then you are a Christian?" asked Franco.

"Yes, I am, and proud of it," Bella said thankfully.

"That is great! So am I," Franco replied excitedly. "I love talking to other Christians

about the Bible. Maybe we can do that sometime."

"Yes, I would like that," Bella replied.

Marianne and Franco said their goodbyes and
turned to speak with another doctor that
walked by.

He was really nice and handsome, too, Bella said to
herself. *Maybe we will see a lot of each other
around here.*

CHAPTER THIRTY-ONE

Bella and Franco did start seeing each other on their days off. They would travel to the other cities, such as Concepcion to see the damage the earthquake had done and determine how they could help the victims there. That was not much of a date, but it did give Bella a chance to know Franco better. The more she knew him, the more she liked him, and it was obvious he was fond of her as well.

"Bella," Franco said as he approached her at the hospital one day, "I have a patient I would like you to meet. He has become a close friend. Daniel Patterson was brought to the emergency room from a construction site accident. A truck hauling debris overturned and some of the rubble fell on Daniel's leg. I was in surgery several hours with him repairing the damage. He is still recovering and is in this bed over here." He was pointing toward the left of the room.

As Bella and Franco approached Daniel, she could see he was a young man in his thirties, medium build, tanned, and blond. He reminded her so much of Evan, the boy who raped her when she was in her teens, but she couldn't think about that now.

"Hi, Daniel," Bella said as she extended her hand. "My name is Bella James and I am a nurse here at the hospital. Franco and I work closely together and he wanted me to say hi to you. I am truly sorry about your accident, but it is a pleasure to meet you."

"The pleasure is mine," Daniel said, as he shook hands with Bella in greeting. "Franco has told me some good things about you also, and I will say he was right about how beautiful you are."

"Well, thank you," Bella said, her face showing a blush, "and what else did he tell you about me?"

"He did tell me you're from Knoxville, Tennessee, and that's where I am from. What a coincidence, don't you think, Ms. Bella?"

"Yes, I do think that's rather strange. But it is a NICE coincidence. People from Tennessee are some of the best people you'll ever meet, right?"

"Oh, I agree completely!"

"We have to go now, Daniel, and check on the other patients. Bella has to get back to Pediatrics. She loves working with the children."

While on a date one evening with Franco, the conversation led to one about Daniel. "Do you know much about Daniel's parents and his childhood, Franco?"

"I know he was adopted immediately after he was born at Baptist Hospital in Knoxville. His birth mother was raped when she was very young and was not able to keep the baby. She thought it best for him to be put up for adoption. The father apparently didn't want the baby. Daniel's parents were killed in a car accident in 2002 while traveling abroad. His adoptive dad was in the construction business and his mother was a school teacher."

"When they died, he inherited some money and decided to travel and reconstruct areas devastated by disasters. He's really a great guy," Franco said.

Bella's heart skipped a beat and she thought to herself, *No it couldn't be! Or could it? Could Daniel be my son? If he is, would he accept me now and forgive me for what I did? Or would he reject me and be very angry?*

"That had to be very hard to lose his parents like that. My heart goes out to him," Bella said. "Do you know when his birthday is?"

"No, but I can look on his admitting papers. Why?"

"Oh, just wondering. I thought I might bake him a cake or do something special for him."

The next day Franco contacted Bella with the date of Daniel's birthday. "It is May 24, 1972," he said.

Bella gasped knowing that is the day her son was born.

"Thank you, Franco," she said. "I appreciate it very much. See you later."

Bella was stunned. Now what would she do?

She prayed that night, *Lord, please let this man be my son and please help him to accept me as his mother and forgive me for what I did.*

The next day, Bella decided she had to try to find out if Daniel really was her son. She phoned the Baptist Hospital in Knoxville because she knew the nurse still worked there that helped with the adoption.

"Good morning, Baptist Hospital. How may I direct your call?" the receptionist sang out.

"I'd like the Obstetrics department, please." Bella pecked her fingers on the table as she waited for the call to be transferred.

"Obstetrics, nurse's station. How may I help you?"

"May I speak to Martha Rivers, please?" Bella asked.

"One moment," said the nurse.

Within seconds, Martha answered the phone.

"Hello, this is Martha."

"Martha, this is Bella Fontaine James. I worked with you for many years. You also took care of the adoption of my baby boy. Do you remember me?"

"Why, of course, I do. How are you doing? It's been a long time. Where are you now and what are you doing?"

"Right now I am in Santiago, Chile assisting Doctors Without Borders with the earthquake victims. There's so much devastation here and so many are in need of medical attention and food. But that isn't why I called," she said quickly.

"How can I help you?"

"Well, it's a long story but I won't go into details. Yesterday I met a young man that is in the hospital here in Santiago. He was injured in a construction accident helping with the rebuilding here," Bella said. "From what I have found out from his closest friend, he may be my son. I really need to know for certain if this is true. Would you please see what you can do to find out about his adoption?"

"What is his name and his parents' names?" asked Martha.

"His name is Daniel Lynn Patterson, birthday is May 24, 1972; and his parents were David and Laura Patterson," Bella said anxiously.

"I'll see what I can find out. Call me back in a few days and I'll try to have the info for you. Okay?" Martha said. "Take care of yourself."

Bella hung up the phone with her hands shaking. She would be in turmoil until she heard something from Martha.

All she could do was wait.

CHAPTER THIRTY-TWO

The next few days seemed enormously long until she could call Martha, but the time finally arrived.

Martha answered the phone. "Bella, I have great news for you!! It's true! Daniel is your son. He was adopted by the Pattersons, who were in their thirties and had been told they couldn't conceive. Mrs. Patterson had previously had endometriosis and it made her infertile. He was in the construction business and she was a school teacher. They were both killed in an auto accident in 2002 when Daniel was thirty years old. It looks as if you may be the only family he has now. Are you going to tell him?"

"Oh, Martha, this is an answered prayer which I have prayed for many years, but God came through in His own time. Thank the Lord!" Bella's mind was spinning. "Yes, I am planning on telling him and hope he will forgive me."

"If he is the man you say he is, he will welcome you with open arms," Martha reassured.

"You're right, and if he isn't, I will find out what he thinks of me. Thanks, Martha, for all you've done."

Bella made a point the next day to have lunch with Franco and give him the wonderful news. She wanted his advice on what to say to Daniel.

"Franco, I have something to tell you about my life that I hope you will understand. We have grown so close and you have become a true friend." She was looking directly into his eyes.

"What is all this mystery, Bella?"

"I am serious about this. Please listen to what I have to say."

"Okay, I'm sorry. I'll listen intently."

"When I was very young, I was raped by a boy I was dating. Soon afterwards, I found out I was pregnant. Since he was the only boy I had ever been with, I knew it was his. My family taught me to have Christian morals and values so I couldn't have an abortion. So I decided to have the baby and put him up for adoption. I didn't want to have anything to do with his father, so I never told him I was pregnant."

"Why are you telling me this, Bella?" Franco asked.

"Well, I have just found out through some research that baby boy is Daniel." Bella had tears in her eyes by this time.

Franco sat back in his seat and gasped.

"I can't believe it! That's wonderful! He's such a great guy and I know he will be thrilled!"

"Do you really think so? Do you really think he'll accept me as his mother now after all these years? Do you think he'll forgive me?"

"Oh, yes, Bella." Franco was overjoyed. "Let's go right now and tell him. May I go with you?"

"Please do and give me some support."

Bella was full of anxiety, not knowing what Daniel would say.

As they walked into Daniel's hospital space, he was lying in bed reading a magazine.

"Hi, Daniel," they both greeted him in unison.

"How are you doing today?" Franco said, "Are you getting through your physical therapy alright?"

"Yes, I'm doing better and PT is going very well. Maybe I'll get to leave this hospital soon."

Bella and Franco couldn't help but smile while talking to Daniel. Daniel knew something was up.

"We have some great news for you, Daniel," Franco said. "You would never guess in a million years what it is."

Bella took a few steps toward Daniel and sat down on his bedside. She took him by the hand and went straight to the point. "Daniel, I am your birth mother."

Daniel was shocked. He sat there for what seemed to be forever, but finally said, "You are! Praise God! I have been praying for this ever since my mother died. I have been so alone. It has to be a miracle that we met like this. What were the chances?"

Bella was so relieved. She looked at Franco and started to sob. "I told you," Franco said, "he is a great guy. She was afraid you wouldn't accept her, Daniel, and be able to forgive her. But you do, don't you?"

"Of course, I do. You did what you thought was best for me. Obviously, you were young and couldn't take care of me, right? I realize that. My parents taught me to always forgive so God would forgive me for my sins. They were great Christian parents. They taught me the Bible and to do God's will in my life. Now we can get to know each other."

Bella sobbed even harder now. She took Daniel in her arms and held him like she had wanted to hold him when he was born. She never got to do that. The nurses took him away from her as soon as he was born. They let her see him but she couldn't hold him. Daniel held onto her, also, both wishing they never had to let go.

Bella spent a great deal of time with Daniel before he was released from the hospital. She had to take care of the children, but made time to visit him.

When Daniel was able to be on his feet, she would take him on walks for his physical therapy. The construction business was his life since he became the Vice President of the company under his dad. His dad was a very successful man, thus very prosperous. His mom taught kindergarten at the elementary school in their community.

Daniel had decided when the earthquake hit Chile he would travel there and work with the reconstruction. He knew the devastation was great and the people had no place to live. He had stayed in a tent while he had been there until the accident. The tent would be his home again after his release.

Bella began telling Daniel about her life and the hard times she had met during her almost 60 years (she never told anyone her age).

Bella and Daniel became very close and stayed in touch with each other often. The mutual love they had grew in such a short time, but no mother and son could have been any closer.

Bella knew she had to share this wonderful news with everybody back in the States. She had to get in touch with LuAnn. Somehow Kathy and Robert had to know, too.

"Hello," Bella said as LuAnn answered the phone.

"Oh, Mom, I am so glad to hear from you. It has been so long. What's happening?"

"I have a lot of great news! LuAnn, I've found my son!! Isn't that great! He's a construction worker here in Chile helping to rebuild the destruction. His adoptive parents lived in Knoxville and he was raised there. I can't believe he was so close and I didn't know it. They were David and Laura Patterson and his name is Daniel. Since he had Christian parents, he's a really great guy. We've grown very close and spent a lot of time together. God has been so good and blessed me more than I could have ever hoped for."

"Oh, Mom, I don't know what to say other than we have been honored with a new family member. I have a stepbrother and I couldn't be happier. When can we meet him?"

"LuAnn, I'll have him get in touch with you when he gets back to Knoxville. I don't know exactly when that will be because he has a lot of work to do here. "

"Also, I have some more good news. The Lord has also given me a good man and I hope he is going to ask me to marry him. He is a Chile native and he is a surgical doctor at the field hospital where I've been working. We have spent lots of time together and have fallen deeply in love. I didn't think I would ever love anyone as much as your father, but I do love him very much. He did surgery on Daniel's leg after he was involved in a construction accident. If it hadn't been for Franco, Daniel would have lost his leg. "

"Boy, you *are* full of news. Anything else? God has truly been blessing you. We are really thankful," LuAnn said.

"I do have something else to ask. Would you do me a favor?" Bella asked.

"Of course, what do you need?"

"I have decided to stay here in Chile because I have faith Franco and I will be married soon. Daniel is here for awhile and it means a lot to me to spend time with him while I have the chance. Also, would you call my employer, Dr. Stanley, and tell him for me? I'm sorry I can't give him a notice but I just can't come back right now. The calls are very expensive from here. Give him my apology. You'll need to call my landlord and tell him I will pay another month's rent then the apartment will be vacant. You're welcome to take any furniture you would like to keep in the family and sell the rest. I won't be able to bring any of it over here. Also, call Kathy and tell her all the news. I would do it myself, but like I said, it costs a lot to call from here. Just remember to give her my love."

"Just please keep in touch with us and let us know how things are going, okay? Know we love you and you are in our thoughts and prayers. Yes, I will take care of everything, don't worry."

"Thank you so much, LuAnn. I'm truly blessed to have you as my daughter. I loved Thomas very much and had a wonderful life with him, but I know he would want me to love again and be happy."

"Call soon, Mom, and tell Franco and Daniel we are anxious to meet both of them," LuAnn said.

"I will; and tell the rest of the family I love them," Bella said.

Little did Bella know God was going to bless her even more in the near future.

CHAPTER THIRTY-THREE

Franco, like Bella had begun to realize that their relationship was growing serious and he also knew they were falling in love. He decided it was time for her to meet his family, so the next morning he phoned his mother.

"Mama', how are you and Papa' doing? There is some good news I want to share with you."

"Hola, my dear son, we are doing fine. What is the news?"

"There is a woman I would like you to meet with whom I am very much in love. Her name is Bella James and she is beautiful, inside and out. When would be a good time for you that I could bring her to your home?" Franco asked.

"We would be happy to meet her anytime, but why not bring her by for lunch Sunday afternoon. Is that okay?"

"That would be great! Gracias, Mama', we will see you soon." It was now Thursday and

Franco made a point to speak to Bella concerning the lunch invitation to meet his parents.

"Bella, you know how much I love you and I know you love me. I think it is time for you to meet my family and give them the chance to care for you as much as I do. Mama' said we could come for Sunday lunch, is that alright with you?" Franco said with excitement in his voice.

"Oh, I want very much to meet your family, Franco. Yes, I do love you and I know I will love them, too. Sunday lunch will be fine. It is an occasion I will look forward to," Bella said, overflowing with emotion.

That Sunday was a beautiful, sunny day in Bella's heart as well as in the Chilean landscape. The undeniable adoration glowed in her smile. Franco's love was strong and sincere and the pride he had for having Bella at his side was candidly observable.

As Franco and Bella drove up the long lane to his parent's home in the countryside outside Santiago, she could perceive how amazing it was. A three story, grey stucco house with countless windows. Terra cotta shutters and trim lined the outside of the structure. As they entered the door, she noticed the brown colored ceramic tile floors which shined like glass. Marvelous huge tapestries hung along the walls like portraits of famous artists. Elegant, brocade drapes covered the long slender windows that led her eyes upward to the high ceilings.

"This is magnificent!" Bella roamed about, taking in the splendor of the entire home.

Suddenly, Franco's parents entered the room.

"Hola," greeted Mrs. Escobar. "I am Franco's Mama'. It is a pleasure to meet you. Welcome to our casa."

"Buenos tardes," Mr. Escobar said, smiling. "My dear, it is so nice to meet you. You are as lovely as Franco said you were. Come sit with us and talk."

Bella and Franco spent the entire day with his family. Evening came quickly and Franco took Bella back to her housing.

"Goodnight, My Dear. See you at the hospital tomorrow," Franco leaned toward her and kissed her passionately. "I love you so much. Will you marry me? I don't have a ring to give you right now but I promise to be good to you."

"Oh, Franco, I don't need a ring. Your love is enough. Yes, yes, yes, I will marry you because I love you, too, with all my heart."

Again, their lips met with ardent intensity.

They felt no need to delay their plans. They went the following day to the Cathedral de Santiago and were wed by the priest there.

Cathedral de Santiago is located on the Plaza de Armes. It is a lovely historical monument. The structure was begun in 1748 and finished 40 years later.

Franco and Bella left the Cathedral with hearts full of devotion to each other, God, and others. Their walk together was to be one yielded to God's will and truly thankful for his blessings.

223

Dear, Lord, you have blessed me beyond words the past months and I am grateful. Thank you, My God and Savior. Amen.

CHAPTER THIRTY-FOUR

The newlywed couple decided to reside with Franco's parents. The home was large enough and Bella loved the idea of living in such an elaborate house. By doing this, they would be able to have the money for future plans which they hoped to put into action soon.

The earthquake victims kept coming into the field hospitals and the staff of doctors and nurses was staying hard at it.

The death toll was escalating from the injuries and hunger. It was a horrifying event and the outside assistance was not coming fast enough, although they were doing all they could.

"Franco, what's going to happen to the children once they are released from the hospital?" Bella questioned with sadness in her voice. "Where will they go?"

Franco looked at her with a lingering frown on his face.

"I don't really know. A few of them can go to the orphanage in Santiago, but there will not be enough rooms to accommodate them all. Let me give this some thought and see what I can come up with."

"Franco," Bella said, "we have to devise a plan quickly. We can't put them back on the streets. As you said, there are still so many that the orphanage won't accommodate. Please come up with an answer."

Bella was deeply troubled about the situation.

All of a sudden, as if a "light" went off in Franco's head, he blurted excitedly, "Oh, Bella, why can't they come live with us? My parents have a huge house with many empty rooms. Mama' and Papa' would be thrilled to have them. Their love for children even surpasses their love for Chile. They would do anything to help. I will talk to them this evening."

Late that afternoon, after work, Franco approached his Mama'.

"Bella and I were wondering where the orphaned children could go to live after they are released from the hospital. There are still many and are no more rooms at the orphanage. We thought it would be wonderful if we could have some of them come live with us here. Would that be okay with you and Papa'?"

"Oh, Franco," said Mama'. "Nothing would make me happier. We could love them and care for them like nobody else. They are God's children and should get the best of attention. That is such a great idea. God Bless you, Franco."

Bella screamed with excitement when she heard the news. She jumped into Franco's arms and gave him a big hug and kiss.

Thank you again, Lord, for taking care of the children and giving us the knowledge and strength to be able to serve them in this way.

The Escobar family made preparations that evening for the accommodations of the orphans. Rooms were cleaned and toys bought to be distributed throughout the home for the assorted ages.

Joy and excitement filled the hearts of the family and servants while awaiting the arrival of the orphans.

CHAPTER THIRTY-FIVE

It is now September 1, 2010 and the weather is very nice. With temperatures in the 50's and 60's, the children were able to play outside and enjoy the countryside, only having to dash in once because of a cloudburst. School teachers were hired to give the children an education.

The children filled the family's every day with love, but it was becoming more and more difficult to find space for all the orphans from the hospital. The other orphanages in Santiago were at maximum capacity.

Bella phoned LuAnn again to update her, first informing her of her marriage to Franco. LuAnn could not have been more understanding or happier for them.

"Another thing," Bella said, "Franco and I have taken in some orphans from the earth-quake into the home of Franco's parents, which is where we're also living.

"Oh, my goodness, Mom! What a thrill, and I'm so happy you were able to help the children. Those are the ones you were never able to birth. Thank God a hundred times for what He has done for you in Chile. That's the best move you have ever made. Your life is finally on the right track and I'm so proud of you."

Things had never been better, Bella thought as she hung up the phone.

After a lengthy discussion, the Escobar family decided, with their resources, it would be the best to build their own orphanage. That way they could accommodate all the children.

For generations, the Escobars had owned grape vineyards and made millions. Although Mama' and Papa' had retired from the business, they still offered help whenever needed. The property consisted of hundreds of acres from which they could choose a perfect location for the orphanage.

Franco began to speak with the architects in the city; Bella was in touch with Daniel to do the construction. It would be wonderful to have him living there while building the orphanage. They could hardly wait to get started.

Every day more and more orphans were coming. The love and affection they gave the children was the talk of the city. Joy and happiness filled the air even with the atmosphere of sadness from the earthquake.

The foundation to The Haven of Joy, the name given the orphanage, was laid on September 10, 2010 and plans were to finish by late November of that year.

Bella made preparations for hiring the employees they would need. They had to hire clerical personnel,administration, cooks, housekeepers, teachers, security guards, maintenance personnel, managers in each department, along with a nurse and a doctor to live on the premises. So an advertisement was put in the local newspaper to interview for the positions.

A retired doctor spotted the ad and called for an interview. Bella gave him an appointment and that afternoon he promptly came to see her.

The servant who answered the door led him to Bella's office. When he entered the open door, Bella thought he looked a little familiar. As he approached her desk, she walked out to greet him with a handshake.

"Hello, Doctor. I'm glad you called for the interview. You're the first to apply for the position," she said, staring into his eyes. "I'm Mrs. Franco Escobar and it is nice to meet you."

What was still familiar about him?

"Nice to meet you, Mrs. Escobar. My name is Dr. Joseph Fontaine. I am originally from Tennessee in the United States but have lived in Chile for 20 years. My specialty is Pediatrics and I love dealing with children. Since I am retired, I don't work in the hospital anymore and would like the opportunity to work here with the children in the orphanage."

Bella stopped in her tracks and sat down in the nearest chair. *I can't believe it,* she thought. *But I knew his voice sounded so much like my dad.*

"Oh, you sound like what we are looking for. Tell me, Dr. Fontaine, do you have children?"

"Yes, I have a daughter named Bella back in the States. I loved her very much but her mother told me to leave them when she was only five years old and to never contact Bella again. I wrote many letters all the years I was gone, but they all came back. She moved and I lost touch with her. It has been my wish for many years to be able to find her with all the new technology we have today. But I don't know if she would want to see me. I haven't been around and she probably thinks I don't love her. But I do love her very much and always have." His sad eyes swelled with salty tears.

He looked at Bella and continued. "Oh, I'm sorry, Mrs. Escobar, I shouldn't be telling you all this. You probably don't care about my personal life. Forgive me."

"Oh, No! I am very interested. You seem like a very sincere man and a fine doctor. I know you will not disappoint us here. You can start the job tomorrow."

"Thank you so much, Mrs. Escobar, and I won't disappoint you, I promise."

Bella knew that he had no idea that she was his daughter and she decided not to say anything for the time being.

Bella was not sure lately how she felt about her dad, though she had prayed for years to see him again. She had, however, always been somewhat angry with him for leaving her. She realized that he told her his letters came back he wrote to his daughter and he lost touch with her later. She could understand that. It would mean her mother didn't want him around and wouldn't let Bella see him. Bella knew now it was not all his fault, but largely her mother's.

Bella woke to a cool September morning and felt she had to tell her dad who she was. As Dr. Fontaine came into the office to report for his employment, Bella asked him to have a seat across from her.

"Dr. Fontaine," Bella began nervously, "I have something I need to tell you."

"Have you decided not to hire me because of my age?" he said.

"Oh, no! That isn't it at all. This is a personal matter. Do you have any idea at all who I am?

Don't you recognize me? My first name is Bella."

Dr. Fontaine's grey eyes grew big and his heart was racing.

"Oh, you can't be!! My Bella, my little Bella? I can't believe it! Oh, Baby, I have wanted to see you for so long. I didn't know if you could forgive me for leaving you. Do you?"

Bella rose from her seat and walked toward him.

"I forgive you, Dad."

They embraced each other and stood there for several minutes, both sobbing heavily.

Again she had to call LuAnn.

That evening was enchanting as if all Bella's dreams had come true. All of her prayers answered. *God is an awesome God!!*

CHAPTER THIRTY-SIX

The day had been a bustling one but Bella and Franco found time to sit alone, outside under the starry skies in the cool of the night. Huddled together, they were wrapped in silence, as if frozen in time. Finally, Bella broke the quiet charm.

"Franco, when I went to Easter Island, I was there to observe the spectacular eclipse of the sun. My life was full of turmoil just like the *darkness* of that eclipse. That thought sent my mind swirling through my life and reflecting upon all of the traumatic times I have known. But during the past few months, the Lord has transformed me and answered many prayers. He has blessed me with a wonderful husband and family who are kind and loving; I have found the other two loves of my life, my son and my father. Also, I have the adoration of children that I wasn't able to give birth to myself, but are just like my own. What else could I ask for? Now my life is like the amazing *brightness* of the emerging sun after the eclipse."

Franco turned and gazed lovingly into her soft, green eyes, a tender smile broadening upon his lips. "Amen, My Love," he said, "amen!!"

Bella was able to witness to many of the victims and children of the earthquake and help them to know Christ as their Lord and Savior.

Two scriptures, among many, Bella will always remember that gave her the strength to get her through her trials are:

John 8:12 (NIV): Jesus said, "I am the light of the world, Whoever follows me will never walk in darkness, but will have the light of life."

Romans 8:28: "And we know that in all things God works for the good of those who love Him, who have been called according to His purpose."

THIS IS THE BEGINNING OF NEW LIFE FOR BELLA-------NOT

THE END